BOUND to CRUELTY

USA Today Bestselling Author
J.L. BECK

New York Times Bestselling Author
MONICA CORWIN

Copyright © 2021 by Bleeding Heart Press

www.bleedingheartpress.com

Cover design by C. Hallman

Cover image taken by Wander Aguiar

All rights reserved.

No part of this book may be reproduced in any form or by any electronic or mechanical means, including information storage and retrieval systems, without written permission from the author, except for the use of brief quotations in a book review.

1
MICHAIL

*A*re we playing babysitter to every fucking mafia princess on the east coast? Waiting in the hall, I catch the last of Kai's phone call, knowing any moment he'll request one of us to take care of this. With Andrea barely functioning and Alexei trying to diffuse his sister, that leaves Ivan and me. Ivan is handling the family's day-to-day business at the moment. I'm the only one who can leave again at the drop of a hat.

Doesn't mean I want to race off and help Kai's sister, the very sister who was supposed to be protecting him and Chicago but left him, and Rose, to rot. She doesn't know the meaning of family and doesn't deserve our protection. So I'll wait, and I won't go unless Kai orders me to, and even then, I might have to think about it first.

Andrea marches down the hall, her dark hair swinging behind her in a shining mass. Today, she's traded her stilettos for black combat boots, which means someone might end up dead. Considering how active Sal's family is, and with the intel she's gathered under her surveillance, it looks like she's ready to take things in her own hands. Adrian told her not to make any moves yet, but I'm in favor of a good...culling. Those bastards need to be wiped out completely. From the grandparents who founded their empire on the blood of children to the cousins who may or may not be involved in the smuggling.

I don't give a shit; they are all going down.

"Michail," Kai calls from his bedroom.

With a sigh, I step into the room and go find him. I have little doubt he's about to send me after his sister. I also have little doubt he won't take no for an answer, even if she seems like a spoiled brat who doesn't deserve his help, or mine.

Even though they share actual DNA, he and I are more family than they will ever be, and for that alone, I'll do what he asks. Hopefully, she'll comply and let me tuck her away into a safe house somewhere to hide until whatever she is dealing with blows over. I suspect, with the season open, she's obviously not equipped to handle things. Someone must have tried a coup and succeeded if she called for an extraction and protection.

So where does that leave our council friends in Chicago then? A good question.

I run my hands through my curls, which are mussed and tangled from all the traveling and wrangling Kai's big body back in one piece. So I leave them instead and walk into Kai's bedroom to take in the scene of domestic bliss.

Rose is turned away, under the covers, asleep by the soft snores I can hear. I shift my focus to Kai. "You need something?"

"Yeah, I need you to go to Chicago and get my sister."

I clench my jaw. "Are you sure about that? She was supposed to be protecting you and didn't do shit, apparently."

Despite lying flat on his back in bed, no shirt, no clothes at all from what I can tell, his tone hardens. "It doesn't matter what she did or didn't do. I don't go back on my word, and if she needs help, she'll get it."

I sit on his bed, careful not to jostle his woman awake. "And what's your secondary plan? How do we keep things cordial with the Chicago council if you're taking her away just after their season opens? What if the new head of the council in her city doesn't take it so kindly?"

"Do I look like I give a shit about council politics?"

I sigh. "You should? This is a game we all have to play now, or each ripple in the pond will send back repercussions."

His gaze turns to ice. "I don't care about your fortune cookie logic. Go to Chicago, get my sister, and keep her safe. That is an order, and as an order, I expect you to follow it without question."

I level him a look. "None of us do anything without question. You know that better than anyone." He nudges his leg over to scoot me off the side of the bed. I stand and dance out of reach before he can do any damage. "I'll bring her back, put her in a safe house, and she'll be fine."

"No, that's not enough. Sit on her until she's safe."

I don't bother asking, *why me*? It would border too close to whining than I'm comfortable with. Instead, I face him, hands on my hips. "Are you sure about this? You want her here? Even after she didn't hold up her end of the bargain, and even though you two don't necessarily get along?"

He stiffens, then grimaces, settling back into his fluffy pillows. "Who says we don't get along?"

"The fact that none of us have met her or anyone in your family. That tells me straight out they are something you want to hide or something you don't think is an active part of your life. So, on that note, is there something about your family I should know, anything about your sister specifically?"

He snorts. "No, and the only reason I haven't introduced any of you is because I consider this my family. They are blood, but you, you are family. And as for my sister, she's a spoiled brat who loves power above all else. Don't let her get under your skin, or she'll burrow deep and cause actual damage."

I nod, and then sigh. "Fine, I'll do as you ask, but you owe me."

His eyes narrow. "What do you want?"

"I want off safe houses and moved to the casino. Alexei can take the safe houses for now; I have an idea about hiding your sister in plain sight."

"At the casino?"

"Why not? Might as well put her to work if she's staying with us."

He moves like he is about to sit up but thinks better of it. "My sister will not be working the bars."

"Really?" I shake my head. "I'm not that big an idiot. I won't force your sister to whore for her room and board, for fuck's sake. Besides, we pride ourselves on women who actually want to be there. Something tells me working at all is a concept your sister is unfamiliar with."

"Just go."

I head toward the door but stop when he calls my name. I wait, listening.

"If you fuck my little sister, I'll kill you."

Wow. I shoot him a glare and don't justify that statement with a response. Like I have time to get my dick wet when every damn heiress needs a protector these days, and the Doubeck family seems to be intent on protecting them all.

No. Right now, all I have time for is packing my bag and calling to get the helicopter ready to depart.

I head to my room and throw open my closet to reveal my stash of weapons on one side, clothing on the other. Everything from tuxedos to rags. There are many parts I've played over the years. Many faces I've worn to secure Adrian's power. Today might call for something a little unconventional. At least until I get the measure of Kai's sister and what kind of danger she poses to us. I'll keep her safe, but only until the moment she puts Adrian and his power base at risk. Then I'll face Kai's wrath, even if he chooses to kill me.

Once I land in Chicago, head to one of our safe houses there, and change, it's time to get to work. With her cell phone signal, the one she used to contact Kai, it's easy enough to trace her. I only hope she was smart enough to use a burner and hasn't contacted anyone else with it.

I find her on the corner of a busy intersection, black, high-heeled boots clicking on the asphalt. Her hood is up, obscuring her hair, but by the way she ambles along, she doesn't seem too concerned. At least not out here surrounded by civilians.

I adjust the pack on my back, pull the brim of my Chicago Cubs hat lower over my brow, and follow her and the mass of people into the subway. I'm very good at preparing for a stakeout. I've already loaded my metro card, and it's easy enough to follow her onto the platform. While she may be a small woman, five-foot-five in those boots, she has a presence of power about her I've learned to recognize in others.

She'll need to strip that away, too, if she plans to stay safe out here in the open. Moving quickly, she gets on the train and finds a stance next to a doorway, her hand gripping the upper rail. I keep my distance, but my eyes stay on her through the crowd, the black sunglasses ensuring she doesn't see me watching her.

After a moment, she turns her face toward me, and I'm shocked she actually picks me out of the crowd. On a whim, I touch the brim of my hat, acknowledging her attention. This causes her to narrow her eyes and face out the window despite the fact it's pitch black in the subway tunnels surrounding us.

When the car slows, she shoves through the crowd to reach me, stopping at the door I've parked myself near. "If you are with them, tell them to fuck off and leave me alone. You won't kill me here in front of all these people."

I scan the crowd. "A knife to the gut takes seconds, and no one will see a thing except the student who tried to help you before the cops showed up, and he got scared."

Her dark eyes flare with something...anger...maybe. It's not fear. I know that much.

She leans in close, and I feel the barrel of a gun through her hoodie pocket. "Try it, asshole, but you're going to have to get a lot of blood on you to keep me from taking a shot before you can get away."

I reach out and grab her hand, shifting the muzzle toward the crowd. "I'm not here to kill you."

"Oh, then what? I know they sent you, so you are here to what, bring me back, beat me up to scare me away?"

Her voice is low, and to anyone else, it might look like we are chatting, flirting even, so I lean into that, dipping my face so my mouth is near her neck. "I'm only here on surveillance at the moment, but the second it's time to do my job, I'll let you know first."

She flexes her jaw, and I catch a whiff of her perfume, something obscenely expensive and frivolous. "Fine, now unhand me. I have to get off."

I chuckle. "Well, I can't help you with that either."

She drags her eyes up to my face and then stops at the sunglasses. "You just made a comment about stabbing me, and now you are joking about giving me an orgasm? Wow. You must be some kind of psychopath."

I lean in again. "The best kind of person, in my opinion."

This earns me a curl of her lip, and she turns to face the door, her shoulder almost brushing my chest. "By the way, you aren't fooling anyone into thinking you're a student. Your shoes are too expensive and that watch screams money. Next time, try a department-store Timex if you want to blend in properly."

The train jerks to a halt, and she steps off onto the platform. I let her go, then follow with the crowd and keep my distance. She doesn't look back, even when she leaves the station and heads north on another crowded boulevard.

I stand near an alley and watch her walk up the steps to a brownstone, unlock the door, and go inside.

Then, I catch someone else peel themselves out of the shadows of her lower stairs and march up to the door. I'm already moving when I catch his profile in the light. What the hell is he doing here? It's the councilman, the same man who helped us free Kai.

What could he possibly want with Selena?

2

SELENA

I lock the doors—the outer set which leads to the street, the inner set on the solid door leading into the foyer, and the living room. It's a beautiful safe house, one I've cultivated over the years through my real estate contacts, but right now, it's not making me feel very safe. Not after the almost altercation with the stranger on the subway. The hardest part is I didn't recognize the man. At the very least, the ones who came for me in my own home, breaking in and attacking me, I recognized as fellow councilmember goons.

This man, who hid behind his hat and sunglasses, I have zero reference for, and I'm good at remembering faces.

I throw myself on the couch and unzip my boots, letting them fall to the floor before I flex my toes in the soft rug, stretching them, rolling my ankles, working out the tension in my calves. I hate wearing heels most of the time, but they are the only thing that gives me a bit of height. Even a few inches can go a long way in a world dominated by men. If they see me as smaller, fragile, they won't listen, and it leads to little *misunderstandings* like we have now.

This is my second season opening. The first one had been uneventful, but the minute this one opened, things imploded.

Someone tried to take my life, and now I'm on the run. How did so many things change in such a short amount of time?

If I were a less confident woman, I'd worry about my position as head councilwoman here.

But I don't do pity parties, and I sure as shit don't let some assholes take what's mine without consequences.

For now, I'll let them think they won, and when the time is right, I'll strike back, decimate them so hard they won't even think about coming for me and mine again.

Once I finish stretching my calves, I strip off the black hoodie, toss it on the chair, and enter the kitchen. I ate earlier, a quick bite while I surveilled the bastard who thinks to take my place. Now, all I need is a bubble bath and a very big glass of wine.

I grab a bottle of white from the wine cooler and a clean glass from the counter. Now set up, I open the bottle, pour about half into the oversized glass, and take one long draw of liquid. It's a little bitter on the back notes, but refreshing, and most importantly, it'll give me a little buzz and hopefully allow me to get some sleep. Something I don't do well without pharmaceutical or alcoholic assistance.

Armed with my wine, I strip off my jeans and head back into the living room in just my black tank top and boy short panties. There's little chance I'll be leaving again, so I should at least be comfortable if I'm going to stare at the ceiling for the second night in a row.

I settle on the couch, lying down, the glass of wine perched on my belly, my hand cradling it gently. But I barely have time to regulate my breathing when someone knocks on the door.

I sit up and take one long draw of the wine before shuffling across the room to grab my hoodie, or more specifically, the small gun in the front pocket.

There's another knock, this one more insistent. I shouldn't have visitors. This is a safe house. No one knows it exists except the former owners, and they are currently on a sailboat exploring the Florida coastline.

I open the first door, then creep into the vestibule, careful not to make a sound. Someone pounds on the door this time.

"Open up, please."

There's something familiar about that voice, but I can't place it.

"No thanks, go away," I call back.

There's a scuffling sound on the concrete steps and quiet again. "Open the door, Selena. No one out here will hurt you."

That doesn't sound very comforting. Especially since the way he worded it made it seem like there's more than just him. "I'll open the door, but if you or anyone else makes any sort of move, I'll shoot, no questions asked."

The voice drips bored, pampered princess. "Fine."

I crack the locks then step behind the door, open it, pointing my gun at whomever is about to walk in. The first is a well-dressed man I don't recognize. The second is holding a gun to his back, and it hits me like a jolt of lightning. It's the man from the subway.

I cradle my wine to my chest and keep the gun pointed at the second man. He seems like the bigger threat. "What do you want?"

He kicks the door closed with his heel and tilts his head to indicate he wants me to go in ahead of them.

I don't take orders from people, especially not assholes who threaten to stab me. "Excuse me. This is my house. I don't know this man, and I don't give a shit if you shoot him. Holding a gun on him bears no threat to me."

"Then why are we arguing instead of going inside where it's warm?"

Goosebumps trail down my legs, making me shiver and reminding me I'm not wearing pants. "Fine."

I lead them both into my living room and give it a sad look. It's a beautiful home, but now that others know it exists, I'll have to move to another place. I face the men again. The well-dressed one with his perfectly coiffed hair looks calm, serene even, as he stands with his hands crossed in front of him. I point the gun at him. "You. What do you want?"

He smiles. A slick, smarmy split of his lips I know all too well. It's the smile of a man about to unload a bunch of bullshit. And it's a little wasteful to see it on such a pretty face. "I'm here to offer you sanctuary on behalf of my council."

I snort, remembering how my brother's bid for sanctuary turned out. This man can't protect me anymore than I could protect my own flesh and blood. "Sanctuary means shit to my council or yours. The second the season opened, and all hell broke loose, my council broke their word when they refused to protect my brother. I don't trust my city's current leadership—or yours. No matter where you are from."

He opens his hands, palms out, the picture of propriety. More like the doodle of delusion. He tops it all off with a glaze of sticky earnestness which might work on someone not raised to detect lies of all kinds, but not me. Even when they are spoken from plush lips and sculpted cheekbones. "Your council didn't protect your brother, but I did. I even helped smooth over some trouble to get him to safety when he was taken captive by our former head councilwoman." He tilts his head toward the other man. "This one can tell you. He was there."

The second man lowers his gun and tucks it into a holster under his arm. Then he strips off his sunglasses and hat. His black curls are smushed down from the ball cap, but without the disguise, he looks almost...beautiful.

I blink, staring between them. "I'm confused."

The councilman speaks first. "This one is a friend of your brother, whom I assume he sent to keep you safe. I, however, am offering long-term protection. Align with me, join our councils, and we will be unstoppable."

I sink onto the coffee table, and both men's eyes drop to my bare thighs. Instead of scolding them, I take another long drink from my wine glass. "I don't know you, either of you, so I don't trust you. But I do know I won't be doing much in line with my duties as head councilwoman until I can retake my seat."

The councilman smiles. "Well, I wish you luck." He moves forward, and the guy behind him has his gun on the councilman faster than I can detect, finger on the trigger. The councilman slips a business card into my hand and backs toward the door.

On the outside, he gives nothing away, but I've lived in this cesspool for years. Each little twitch, the beads of sweat on his temples, even the slight tremor in his fingers as he passed me his card gives him away. He might pretend to be unmoved by a gun to the back of his head, but he's anything but.

He's gone before I even have a chance to find out how he found me, how he found this place. Which means it's no longer safe. Damn it. I'm already tired of running, and I haven't even started yet.

I eye the second man. "And you? Are you here to kill me or protect me?"

He dumps his backpack on the floor and then his coat on top of it, his eyes roaming the room. "That man wasn't lying. He helped us get your brother to safety after our head councilwoman went all *Misery* on your brother. He's at home now, resting and recovering from a likely drug overdose."

I'm on my feet and heading toward my burner phone before I think about it. But once I start dialing, the other man snatches it from my hand, drops it on the floor, and stomps on it. "That's not safe to use."

He digs another device from his pocket and hands it to me. "Just hit number one, and it will autodial to Kai."

I grind my teeth at his high-handed tone but do as he says because I want to speak to my brother. He answers on the second ring. "Michail? Are you there yet?"

"It's not your friend, just me."

"Selena, good. I'm glad he reached you. You called for help, and I sent the best."

I refrain from telling him his *best* threatened to stab me. "What am I supposed to do here? I can't leave the city, or I can't fight to get my seat back."

His tone is arctic, even through the phone, and I shiver. "You didn't ask for help to secure your council seat; you asked for sanctuary. I'm providing it, but you have to go with Michail. Those are my terms."

He's reminding me I refused him protection once upon a time. Maybe he's more my brother than I've given him credit for. "Fine, but once I'm safe, I will return to take back what's mine."

"I'd expect nothing less from you, little sister."

I hang up and toss the phone back to the other man—Michail. "So, he says we are going somewhere?"

His gaze shifts around the room. "Let me take a look around first, and then we'll go. Also, it might give you time to sober up."

I chug back the rest of the wine while I lock eyes with his. "It takes a lot more than this to get me drunk."

Gently, I set the glass on the coffee table and throw myself on the couch. If he's here to protect me, I might as well try to get a little sleep before we leave.

When I lie down, he moves out of my line of sight to do God knows what. The last few days seem to close in on me, and within a few minutes, I'm dozing.

Until someone shakes my shoulder hard enough to nearly drag me off the edge of the couch. I jerk awake in one of those full body muscle-tensing moments and glare at him. "Really? I haven't had a full night's sleep in days, and you are going to wake me up now?"

He kneels by the couch, his eyes almost even with mine while I'm sitting. "Let's get one thing straight to start out. I don't work for you. Hell, I barely work for your brother. Adrian is the only one who pulls these strings. You so much as take one step out of line, I'll find a nice retirement community to stash you away. You can spend your days eating frozen meals and playing bingo until someone eventually figures out where you are and finishes the job they started."

I rub the sleep from my eyes. "For fuck's sake, just give me a second to wake up."

A bag lands beside me on the couch. My bag from the look of it. "We are leaving in ten, so I suggest you get it together and be ready to walk out the door when I am." His tone is dead serious, no give, none of the joking man I met on the subway.

It's almost as if... "You don't like me, do you?"

He stands and heads toward the door. "I think you're a spoiled brat who doesn't know how good she has it." His eyes dip to my lap. "And I think you should put on some fucking pants before we leave."

3

MICHAIL

We aren't even out of the city yet, and I want to turn around and dump the brat on her enemy's doorstep. I can easily see why someone would be after her, especially if her attitude translates into her leadership skills.

I sit back in the car's seat and ignore her as she continues to complain, as she has been doing since the first moment she woke up an hour ago. She complained we drove instead of flying, complained the car was too hot or too cold. She complained she didn't have the proper support for her back to sleep in the SUV.

Hell, I don't think there is a single thing she hasn't complained about—especially me.

I pound my forehead against the chilled window a few times and turn to look at her. "If you don't shut the hell up, I'll gag you for the duration of this trip."

She stiffens, her back going even straighter than before in her princess posture. "You wouldn't dare. You can't treat me like that. I'm a—"

"Pain in my ass? Job I don't need? One tongue too many for someone who isn't a corpse?"

Her eyes go wide, and she clamps her lips shut.

"That's fucking better." I settle into my seat again and stare out the window. Only another hour until we reach the city, and I can get some much-needed sleep. It will be at the casino, but I can survive. The princess might not be able to though.

Thankfully, she gets the hint and stays quiet until we pull up outside the casino. I check my guns and pull on my ball cap. "Stay in front of me, don't wander, and don't gawk. The faster we get you up to the room, the safer you'll be."

She scans my face; hers is the picture of control. Something I can appreciate, even if it makes my job harder. "You think they will take a shot at me in a crowded casino?"

I shrug. "I have no idea what they will do, since I'm not sure who is after you yet. We'll take this one step at a time, and the first step is getting you out of the public and secluded."

"Why did I have to leave Chicago for that? I was perfectly secluded in my safe house."

I shove the door open, march around the car, and yank her door open too. "You mean the safe house that I and another city's councilmember located? Yeah, super safe."

This time, she curls her lip, rolls her eyes, and slides out of the SUV, wobbling in her ridiculous heels. I point to them. "First thing that goes are those shoes. How can you run for your life if you can't even move properly? You're more likely to break an ankle than escape."

She tosses her long dark hair over her shoulder. "Oh, honey, I can run in any shoes, heels or not. You don't know shit about me, so stop making grand assumptions and take me to my room so I can get some proper rest."

It's on the tip of my tongue to rebuke her for calling me honey, but I decide to pick my battles, and knowing the war I'm about to face, her nicknames are trivial.

I nod at the driver and close the SUV door. In the second I took my eyes off her, she already started into the casino. I catch and grab her arm, pulling her into my chest. "What part of stay in front of me don't you understand?"

We make it to the room before I have to throw her over my shoulder and drag her, which I'm inclined to do if she keeps fighting me at every turn. For now, we need to get inside and have a come-to-Jesus moment.

I lock the door behind us, and she turns to look at me. "You can leave. This will do fine."

Wow. I blink and then blow out a long breath to gain some patience. "Well, Princess, this room is for both of us. How the hell am I supposed to guard you if we aren't in the same space?"

She waves at the windows across the room. "You think my attackers are ninjas who can climb twenty stories?"

I move in closer, finally entering the hotel room and crowding her into backing up. "No, but I think your attackers can afford to bribe a bellman, a cook, a maid, anyone who can slip in here with a knife or poison. I can't combat threats if I'm not here. That is way more fucking explanation than you deserve, so sit down, shut the fuck up, and let me tell you the rules."

I back her to the leather club chair near the bed as we speak, then gently shove her into it. She sputters, but I crouch in front of her and slowly shake my head. Thankfully, she stays silent, even if she glares the entire time. "You are under our protection now, and you called us for help, so we do this my way. There are no ifs, ands, or buts. If I tell you to do something, you do it. If I tell you to jump, you say…"

"How high?" she deadpans, crossing her arms under her breasts.

"No, you don't say a goddamn word. You just start jumping. Got it? Anything I require from you will be for your own safety, so I won't take questions, comments, or complaints."

She digs through the bag on her lap and unearths a cell phone still in its wrapper. I watch while she fumbles with the packaging, takes it out, and dials a number. After a moment, all I hear is ringing until the phone goes dead. No option for a voicemail. She tries again with the same results.

"I don't know who you are calling, but if it's anyone other than God himself, there's nothing you can do to change what's happening."

She tosses her phone into her bag angrily. "I didn't ask for help just to be abused."

I peel the sleeve of my jacket up to show her thin white lines in equal rows down my arm from wrist to elbow. "This. This is abuse. You don't know the meaning of pain, of hardship, not up there in your ivory tower. You don't know what it means to sell yourself, body and soul, for safety. But I assure you, you will by the time I'm done."

She stares at my scars, blinks, and looks at my face, her eyes softening. "How?"

I pull my sleeve down and stand. "We don't have time for stupid questions. I'll show you to your room."

"Oh, you're allowing me to have my own room? How generous."

I ignore that comment. She can run her mouth all she likes as long as she listens to me.

Inside the room is a short woman sitting on a chair who scrambles to her feet when we enter. "They to-to-told me to wait in here. I'm ready when you are."

I ignore her, too, and lead Selena to the bed. There's a red dress on the coverlet, exactly like the house girls wear when they are working. It's short, but well cut, and definitely highlights a woman's assets, no matter her size. "Put this on. Then we'll do something about your hair."

Instead of taking the dress, she hikes her backpack up on her shoulder, spins toward the door, and walks out. I wait a moment and follow, not really sure what she's doing now.

She's already halfway out the room door by the time I grab her around the waist. I easily lift her off her feet, snag her bag before it hits the floor, and throw her over my shoulder. She pounds on my back with her fists, but it's insignificant.

I nod to the hairdresser. "We need a moment, please."

She scrambles out and closes the bedroom door behind her.

I toss Selena on the bed and take great pleasure in watching her scramble around to get upright again. "You fucking bastard. You don't touch me."

Oh, really? I lean over her, putting my weight into it, forcing her back on the bed until I'm almost on top of her. Now she's breathing heavily, panting, her eyes blazing.

"I can do whatever the hell I want, when I want, and if you have a problem with it, then you can explain to your brother, and your whole family, how you were too precious to let me keep you safe."

She purses her lips, all anger and bite now. "Get off me."

"Are you done with your little hissy fit?"

When she glares, I lie on top of her fully, pinning her small body beneath my bigger one. "I take that as a no, Princess."

She tries to shove at my shoulders, but she doesn't do any damage. It's not until she stills do I finally peel myself off her body and let her sit up.

"Was that really necessary?" she asks.

It's my turn to glare. "I don't know, was it? Tell me you agree to my conditions, and we can go from there."

She juts her chin up at me, looking down her nose. Something she no doubt has a lot of practice with. "Fine, I agree, but you aren't doing shit to my hair. Please."

"Fine, as long as you agree to help me in return. Wear the dress and help me in the casino. Consider it work for room and board."

This time she snorts, a petulant little smile on her mouth. "I can just pay you. How about that? I'd rather do that than wear whatever the fuck this dress is."

I pick up the dress and toss it in her lap. "Too bad you just agreed to my rules, and we made a deal. You listen to me, and I'll keep you safe. In turn, I won't touch your appearance unless it's vital to keeping you safe, and you help me on the casino floor."

She narrows her eyes, holding the dress up to get a better look at it. "Doing what? I'm not spreading my legs to keep you from cutting my hair. That is not ensuring my safety in the slightest."

"Did I say you'd be working the floor that way? No. But everyone who works here is going to think that. You will blend in with the other girls, make yourself positively unnoticeable if you can manage it, and we'll work together to figure out who is trying to kill you."

The hairdresser pokes her head back in. "Can I leave or..."

I wave her away. "Go, but don't tell anyone you were up here."

She scrambles away, and I hear the front door close with a heavy thud a few seconds later.

"There, she's gone. You got your way this time."

She wads the dress and tosses it on the bed. "Fine, but I need to get some sleep right now. It was a long night of riding in that car, and I didn't get any."

I head toward the door, my back to her. "Maybe if you stopped complaining long enough and closed your mouth, you might have gotten some."

"Fuck you," she calls.

I turn and face her. "Fuck you back. I don't like you, you don't like me, and that is fine. We don't need to be friends to make this work. So, keep your shit together. I'll do the same, and the second I can unload your ass back to your brother, we part ways for good."

I make it to the doorway, but she says my name, which makes me pause since I couldn't remember if I told her or not.

I glance over my shoulder at her, waiting for her to speak.

"You got your way this time, but I won't be so easily manipulated again."

To that, I only smile and close the door behind me as I go.

4

SELENA

I got myself into this mess.

Worse—I throw myself back onto the bed and cover my face with my hands—I asked for this "help." Does my brother know how his friend is treating me? Would he even care after I let him down so royally when he came for my help? Maybe sending Michail to fulfill his promise to the letter in the most painful way possible is payback,.

I shove the dress farther away from me and groan before heaving myself up again to find my toothbrush, face wipes, and pajamas. I need sleep, and I need it badly. Who knows what my new protector has in store for me? I can't risk being off my game from too little sleep when it's time to find out.

When I exit the bathroom, freshly washed and ready to climb into bed, the dress mocks me. It screams "you did this to yourself" as if I haven't already figured that out.

If I grabbed my belongings and walked out the door right now, would he let me go, or has he already created some grand scheme in his mind? From what little I've seen of him, he's definitely a planner.

I grab my dirty clothes and place them near my suitcase while I consider Michail. Kai and I haven't spoken a lot over the past few years. Even less since I took over the council. So everything I know of his friend has been gleaned since he stalked me on the subway.

Thinking back, he'd been very good at finding me, at blending in despite his almost otherworldly beauty. The man has bone structure made for movies or modeling, and yet he hides it, keeps himself hunkered down and hidden. An interesting dichotomy which I need to figure out lest it be used against me later.

I climb into bed and settle the covers over my lap just as the door opens, and he walks in.

"Don't you kn—" The words die in my mouth as I get a look at him.

He carries a tray with food and a glass of water to the end of my bed and leaves it. But it's not the food that's left me dumbstruck. It's the low sling of his cotton pajama pants outlining his bottom half. All of his bottom half. Also, all the bare skin above since he's not wearing a shirt. He doesn't have any tattoos that I can see, but there are scars all over him in various shades of white and pink, also various sizes. He's riddled with them but doesn't seem concerned about hiding them from me.

Just as I don't bother hiding as I slide my gaze down his torso to the sharp cut of his hip bones and back up again. Goodness gracious. He plays the chameleon even better than I'd given him credit for if he hides all this muscle under his clothing where no one's the wiser.

I croak out, "Thanks."

This makes him narrow his eyes at me, but he says nothing as he turns and walks out.

His back. I blink, taking in the lines and marks across his skin. Scars from being whipped, but I can't tell with what. So he hadn't lied about knowing abuse firsthand. No one would submit to something like that willingly.

When my door closes, I think about racing over and locking it, but I doubt it will keep him out, so I don't bother.

I grab my phone and try to call my brother again. This time he deigns to answer, and I sit up from where I'd slumped back into the pillows. "Kai? Is that you?"

"You called me, Selena. Who the hell do you think is answering my phone?"

I huff, exhaustion taking hold. "You didn't answer the phone earlier when I called, so how the hell am I supposed to know what you will or won't do?"

There's an edge to his tone when he shoots back. "What do you want? You asked for help, and I sent help. If you're unhappy with the arrangements, you can handle things on your own like you usually do."

I tense. On my own. Like I usually do.

He's not wrong. I don't ask for help unless I'm already ten feet in quicksand and likely about to drag anyone who helps down with me. It's disconcerting that he knows me so well after all these years, while I feel like I don't know him at all.

Either way, his voice, and hell, his words too, are telling me to fuck off. That he's done his duty as a family member and can't be bothered anymore.

I don't know why it hurts, but it does. Nothing should hurt anymore. Not after everything I've done to get where I am, after everything I've given up.

So, instead of arguing with him, I nod to myself since he can't see it anyway. "It's nothing. Just wanted to say I'm safe for now, I guess."

"Great," he says, his tone tight, the word rushed. "If you need anything, ask Michail. He might be a hard-ass, but he'll make sure nothing happens to you."

He hangs up without waiting for me to say goodbye.

I slap my phone on the bedside table again and eyeball the food. I'm not hungry. And there's no way I can sleep after barely talking to Kai. Or with that stranger in the next room doing god knows what, planning ways to make me miserable while he is on babysitting duty.

I throw off the covers and walk to the empty space in the center of the room, a wide space leading from the bed to the door, then take a deep breath, bring my arms over my head, and fold down to touch my toes. Yoga seems silly to a lot of people, but it helps me, so I do it when I need to.

I spot the door open again while my head is down, my fingers stuck underneath my feet.

He skirts around me slowly, as if he's trying to figure out what I'm doing.

"Yoga," I supply. "It's called yoga."

He's still not wearing a shirt, and seeing him again, this time closer to me, is as distracting as it was the first time. He smells like lemongrass and coffee. His hair sticks up in curly puffs like he's been running his hands through it.

"I know what yoga is."

I straighten and bring my arms up again, repeating my initial motion, bending down to fold. "Great. What do you want?"

He waves to the tray on my bed. "To make sure you ate something, but it doesn't look like you have."

"No, I'll eat it when I wake up. I need to sleep more than anything right now, which is what I'm trying to do."

This time, he doesn't try to mask his contempt. "You think stretching will help you get to sleep?"

I shrug and tuck my hands under my feet again, bending my knees slightly since they are still sore from fighting with the assholes who broke into my house. "At the very least, it keeps me from murdering you in your sleep. So for now, you should be grateful for it."

His eyes lock on my backside where my shorts have ridden up. "Sure, whatever."

I stand and shake out my limbs, then sit on my bed since he won't allow me to focus on the yoga, the sleeping, or the eating apparently. "Did you need something?"

A line forms in the middle of his forehead, and he steps closer, bringing the scent of him closer too. "Yes, actually. I also wanted to know why you think the council is trying to oust you as its leader."

"Why I think or why they actually are doing it are two different things."

His gaze bores into mine. "I'm aware of that. Answer the question."

It's not simple. I've thought about this since the initial attack. Why do they want me out? I'm not a bad leader. Yes, I can be a bitch, but I keep things running smoothly, money in everyone's pockets. Maybe someone thinks it's not enough. I shake my head, not meeting his eyes since I don't want him to see my weakness—that there are many things I don't know. "You probably have a better theory than me. Everyone on my council seemed content before this happened. Everyone in society, all of it was perfectly normal as of a couple of days ago. The second Kai and Rose left town things went to shit fast. At first, I thought it was him, paying me back for not doing enough to help him..."

"Not doing enough?" he interrupts. "From what I can tell, you didn't do shit to help him or Rose."

I keep my mouth closed because I don't disagree with him. Did I try to help my brother? Yes. Did the bitch of a councilwoman here block me at every turn? Also, yes. It was like a race across a pitch-black room with no help, and my opponent had a flashlight and a map. Kai knew the threat he was facing; I hadn't realized it was so dire until it was too late.

"Nothing to say to that?" he asks, dragging me from my thoughts.

I'm tired, and it's weighing me down now. "What do you want me to say? You have already made up your mind based on what you think you know. From what I've already learned of you, I won't be able to change it, so why bother?"

He narrows his eyes and takes a step toward me. It doesn't matter if he wants to hit me or hurt me or harm me. I can't do a thing about it until he makes his move. There's no point in acting until that moment, so I don't.

I stare at him from my place on the bed, and I wait. I wait for him to slink closer, thinking he has the upper hand. When he's close enough I can feel his body heat, he doesn't do anything but stare down at me. "You look like him."

It's not the response I'm expecting, and the surprise of it startles me into answering honestly. "We all look like our parents."

"Where are they?"

If Kai hasn't told him about our parents, I don't see a reason to explain them. Besides, many don't understand my choice of life, my sibling's choice of life, after we grew up in the least bad of society homes. We were fed, clothed, cared-for. So many people our ages didn't even have those basic necessities. By the spark in Michail's eye, I'm thinking he's one of those unfortunate ones.

"Don't look at me like that," he says, his voice taking on a deeper note, huskier, edged with darkness, dipped in displeasure. "I don't need pity from a spoiled mafia princess. Definitely not one who grew up with the perfect family in the perfect life."

I keep the questions out of my voice. "No one's life is perfect. Stop assuming you've put together the entire puzzle just because you found the corners."

There's no point in trying to get to know this man when he ensures I know how he feels about me as often as he can. He thinks he knows everything about me from what, reading my dossier, from knowing my brother? He hasn't even scratched the surface of who I am, or what I'm capable of. And he doesn't want to. Which begs the question...why is he here, standing in front of me, so angry, asking me things he really doesn't care about?

I slide back into the bed and settle against the pillow. "Did you need something else? If not, I'm going to sleep. It's been a long day."

His eyes slide over me one more time, and then he storms out, slamming my door behind him.

5

MICHAIL

I decide, after our little chat this morning, to leave her alone for a while. She's not like I expected, and it's thrown me. I don't like when people don't fit into the boxes I've assigned them. With her, I thought I'd figured her out pretty quickly, but now, I'm not so sure.

I still can't stand her, but I'm thinking there's more under the surface than a pretty princess playing at being a queen. It would make sense given what I know about Kai and the friendship we've built over the years. With him, things are often far more complicated than expected.

So I bring her food, leaving it outside her door with a knock, and I wait. Later tonight, we'll be heading down to the casino to get to work, but right now, I'm itching to know what it is about her I'm not quite grasping.

When the sun sets, I walk into her room without knocking. She's propped on the bed, her dark hair in a messy bun piled high on her head.

I stop at the edge of her bed and stare down at her, but she barely spares me a glance. "Can I help you?"

It's the high-handed way she says everything that seems to burrow under my skin, bringing up my anger from the depths. "Yes, actually. It's time to get dressed and hit the floor. I have some work to do, and you're coming with me."

Her eyes jump toward the end of the bed where the dress is laying. "Do I really have to wear that?"

I shouldn't be pleased by the misery in her voice. "Yes, you really do. It's the uniform, and I want you to blend in."

"I can't blend in wearing my own clothes? Even if I let you pick the outfit?"

I point toward the bathroom door. "There are some toiletries and cosmetics in the bathroom. If you need anything else, please let me know. I'll see what I can do. Meet me by the door in an hour."

To my surprise, in one hour exactly, she walks out of her room wearing the dress, matching shoes, her makeup perfect, her hair…I swallow hard and close the distance between us, even though she's not anywhere near the door.

"We need to do something about this hair." I spin her to face her bedroom door and gather her long mass of dark hair into a low ponytail. Then I spin it into a hefty low bun, fish the spare ballpoint pen from my inner suit pocket and secure it. The scent of jasmine wafts from her hair, forcing me to step away from her, to shut it off.

She fans her fingers over the bun. "I don't think that will hold very long."

"Well, it's what we are working with right now. Your hair is distinctive, it's…" I stop myself from saying beautiful. "I said you need to blend in, so…try harder."

She waves at the dress, her lips folded down into a thin line. "I am wearing what you gave me. I followed your directions. If you want me to blend in better, let me wear my own clothes."

"No, for now, you wear this. When we get more of a threat assessment, maybe you can wear something else."

I turn to the door, throw it open, and wait for her to exit into the hallway. She walks out, and I lead her toward the elevator and slap my palm against the down button. "This won't be easy for you. When I'm down there, I have to play the part of one of Adrian's Five. I know you already know what that means. You will have to play the part of my possession. So right now, start getting it through your thick skull that I own you."

She stares at the elevator doors like she might melt the steel with her eyes. "No one owns me, but I can pretend for a little while."

"That will be fine for now. Keep your head down, don't leave my side, and if you hear or see anything that sets off an alarm bell, tell me immediately. Anything. I don't care if it's a tingle up your arm, or you lock eyes with a man, and your pussy gets wet. If something is off, I need to know."

Her gaze is ice when she shifts it to my face. "What does, or does not, make me wet is none of your concern. But I'm perfectly capable of keeping you apprised of any threats I notice."

The elevator stops, we step inside, and I hit the casino button this time. She shifts to the back of the elevator, leaning on the bar. I turn and pull the knob to stop the elevator, then face her.

Her gaze glides from my chest, in the custom charcoal suit Kai gave me for my birthday, up to my mouth, then my eyes. "Why are we stopping?"

I take one step forward, entering her space, something I've been careful about. Jasmine hits me again, just like before, and I cup the back of her neck to tilt her face up toward me. "You are playing the part of my lover. Touch me here, now, so it doesn't seem awkward when we are out there."

She fiddles with her earring for a heartbeat, and I expect an argument, but then she places her hands on my chest, flat, like she's brushing the lint off her clothing. I use my other hand to pull her in tight by the waist, then slide down to the fleshy curve of her ass.

With a satisfying squeak, she jerks against me, her eyes shocked and wide now. Some part of her hadn't expected me to touch her, but for us to be convincing, and I'm always convincing, she needs to own this just as much as I'll have to.

"I know this is distasteful to you, but you need to step it up to ensure your safety. Play the besotted lover, or at the very least, the whore latched on to her favorite wallet. Whatever you need to do to tell the story, I don't give a fuck."

She nods, the set of her shoulders the only revelation of her tension. "Why? Why are we doing it this way, and not like hiding me in a closet somewhere until this all blows over?"

I give her a little smile. She's earned it for not slapping me the second I grabbed her ass. "Because running and hiding isn't my style."

Something enters her eyes, not the questions I've watched her wrangle into submission every time she sees me, but something else. A darker knowledge I wouldn't ascribe to a pampered princess like her. "What is your style?"

I lean in and scrape my teeth along her jaw. She arches into me, and for a second, I think we might pull this off if her reactions stay as genuine as that little shudder I just felt. "I don't run and hide. I lay in wait. I learn everything I can about my enemies, then I strike hard and fast enough that they never see me coming."

She digs her fingers into the back of my neck, leaning her face back as if welcoming my mouth on her skin, as her nails tangle in my hair. "What does that make me? An accomplice or a target?"

I nip her one more time and release her to hit the button on the elevator. Her face is flushed, her cleavage is higher in that obscene little red dress, and she looks thoroughly ready to fuck, as I intended. "I haven't figured that out yet. So I guess for now, you're safe."

The elevator dings, and I hold my arm out for her to take, but she wraps herself around my side, letting me lead her out onto the loud floor.

Immediately, the sounds overwhelm me, but I quickly tune the dings and clinks of the machines and tables out in trade for the voices. People screaming in excitement, in anger, some happy, some intoxicated.

It doesn't matter how many times I walk these floors; I always find the vibrancy of it all a little exciting. Like the carnivals I used to see as a kid and never got to go to. But that's the point. Wind the people up and take their money.

I lead her along the edge of the floor, drifting, as if we have all the time in the world. To her credit, she doesn't stumble along beside me, she clutches me tight, and saunters, exactly as I expect she would if she were walking in front of her people.

When I risk a glance at her face, she's even wearing a slightly dreamy expression, like she can't quite believe what's happening. It'll do, since I rarely even acknowledge our working girls.

We head to the club at the far end of the casino. It'll just be picking up, and I can get a good read on where any action is happening tonight.

I lead her to the bar and signal the bartender. When the man comes over, he gives Selena a strange look, so I sit on the stool and pull her into my lap. She settles and leans into my chest, gathering my hand in hers and threading our fingers together. I toss fifty dollars on the counter and order two whiskeys. Technically, I don't have to pay here, but I'd rather no one who doesn't need the information know who I am.

He places the drinks in front of us and heads off to deal with more customers.

While she's leaning back, giving me access, I trail my mouth down the side of her neck. "We'll relax in the VIP area for a bit, and listen for anything helpful, and then we'll head back upstairs. You won't have to endure this for long."

She wiggles in my lap like she's ready for me to do a lot more than hold her. "Fine, lead the way."

I ease her up, stand, and grab our drinks, pinching the glasses together in one hand, still holding hers in the other. We enter the VIP section, which is almost full already, and find a table near the border of the public area of the club and this more restricted area. It's better to be able to hear things on both sides of the line.

A couple of the real working girls saunter past, swaying their hips, giving me wide Bambi eyes. I should have expected the attention since I don't typically mess with any of them. They probably considered me off limits until now. *Shit.*

I pull her over into my lap again, this time putting her sideways so I can speak to her easily. "See, that wasn't so hard."

She laughs like I've said the funniest thing in the world, then sobers and leans in so our mouths are almost touching. "I'm not an idiot. I get the concept of what we are doing. What I don't get is why I can't be your assistant, or your personal chef, or hell, your valet. Why am I wearing this skimpy red dress and grinding on your lap like I want to go for a ride?"

The visual hits me before I think about her words. I take a second to gain control of myself again. Unacceptable.

I grip her chin, about to set things straight, but her eyes stray to the two girls making another lap, looking like they might come in and see if I want some extra company.

Then her mouth is on mine, her fist in my hair, and I'm tasting her, all before I can process the idea in my brain, assimilate it. She overtakes my senses. The whiskey she sipped, and the cool clear taste of her, like a rainstorm on a hot day. I cup the back of her neck and let her finish what she started.

All too soon, she breaks away and casts sleepy eyes over at the girls. She's marked her territory, and they back off to make their rounds.

When she brings her gaze back to mine, I realize she's shifted so she's straddling me, the back of the dress barely covering her ass, her panties pressed against my slacks, exactly where I'd want her if...

"What was that?" I ask, already knowing the answer but needing the time to get a hold of myself.

She shrugs and wipes her mouth gently. "You said make it convincing." Her eyes go wide, and she looks down at where my erection is tenting my pants. "I guess I made it a little too convincing."

Oh no. I capture her face in my hands and pull her back to me like I might finish our kiss. It leaves me speaking against her wet mouth, my lips brushing hers with each word. "No, Princess. You fooled them, and it will do for now, but this doesn't concern you."

Her brows draw down, and she catches my wrists, one in each hand. "Oh, you're a virgin. That makes so much more sense now."

6

SELENA

I don't know why I felt the need to push his buttons last night. My only reasoning is because he does it so easily to me, and if I find a place to prod, I should do it while I have the chance.

This morning, he doesn't bring me food, so I assume the door service is over. When I get so hungry my stomach rumbles loudly, I slip on the short silk robe I brought and head out of my bedroom to find something to eat. Even if I have to order it.

I find a small breakfast nook set off in a tiny galley kitchen, but it's occupied. He sits in one of the two chairs, a tablet in one hand, a mug of coffee in the other.

His eyes barely scan over me before dismissing me completely. So I sit. If we stay here, together, silently, I can work with it.

There's an extra mug and a carafe, so I pour myself some coffee. What I wouldn't give for some news right now. But I don't care about the headlines. I want to call one of the few people I trust in my city and find out what's happening, who is doing this to me, and how I can stomp them under my stiletto and put things back to normal.

So with none of that, and my captor unlikely to provide any news even if I ask nicely, I consider how maybe I shouldn't antagonize him. And yet, the first thing I want to do is fight with him. His face is too perfect, too smug, and every time he looks at me, it's as if I'm the insect infestation he's unable to get rid of.

I sip my coffee and study his face. Damn. He really is too fucking beautiful for his own good. The women in my city would eat him alive, especially if my speculation about him being a virgin is true. He has to be in his late twenties, so more my brother's age than mine. But there's something about him that makes him seem older. A weight which hangs off his shoulders, dragging them down to the level of someone far more experienced.

By the scars on his body, he's seen things. Terrible things. Maybe that's what makes his eyes look just the wrong side of haunted and his bearing feel so much older.

"Stop staring," he snaps. I jerk and slosh hot coffee over my hand.

With a hiss, I grab a napkin and swipe at it, then set my cup down. "I'm not staring. I'm analyzing."

"Then go analyze something else. I don't need your assessing glances or your surveying stares, none of it. I'm not a man to be fixed or figured out."

I snort. "I have zero interest in fixing you or learning anything about you I don't already know. You're here to keep me safe. That's what I need to know, end of discussion."

"And yet you asked me a far more personal question last night."

I pick up my coffee to hide behind so he can't see the heat in my cheeks. "That wasn't a question; it was an observation. Since you're the one who brought it up, are you a virgin? Will that be a problem for you? Acting like we're spending time together."

The corner of his lip teases upward, and he slides the tablet onto the table. "First of all, I'm insinuating we are fucking, not actually fucking you, so that's none of your business. Secondly, it's not your job to make observations about me."

I sit back in the chair, still cradling my mug. "Fine. Are you investing any energy into figuring out who is hunting me, or should I get dressed and start working on that myself? Lord knows neither of us wants me here any longer than necessary."

He rolls his eyes and pins me with a look. "We started working on that last night."

"Between the drinking, or your erection? When did we get anything useful?"

His jaw tightens. I know I'm pushing him again, and I can't fucking help it. Like poking a viper with a stick and hoping to stay out of range.

"You are such an entitled little brat. For your information, despite my body's response to your very nice ass, and don't worry, that's not a compliment since you already know what you look like and how to wield your looks like a weapon, I was listening to the crowd. As of right now, no one at all is whispering about you, or your little coup." He goes silent, scanning my face. "I'll let you figure out why, for now."

He snatches the tablet off the table again, resetting his light gray suit jacket, and continues to read.

Yeah, I can't keep doing this. If I stay at this table, I'm going to punch him, and I don't entirely trust that he won't hit me back. I grab my mug and some toast off the cold stack in the middle of the table and retreat to my room.

For now, I'll let him think he's won. At the very least, maybe it will keep him off my back for a while.

I put the toast on my bedside table and stare at my phone, considering a call.

My other sister and I don't have the same relationship Kai and I do. She's been my friend, as much as my family, for years. As much as I long to hear her voice, I can't bring myself to make the call. Not when it could get me caught and put her in danger.

As one of society's best assassins, she's always in danger, but she doesn't get involved in political intrigue. In fact, the second she gets a whiff, she runs far, far away, leaving the politics to me and our parents. She'd be able to give me a read on my city, though, feel the tempo and let me know if I have a shot at taking back everything I've worked for over the past couple of years.

I put my face in my hands, knowing the tears are coming, and at least I can hide them away until my weakness passes. Until I get myself under control again.

Thinking about it makes things worse. I've lost everything. My parents trained me to lead the council, and I did. But now, without that, what am I? What the hell will I do with my life if I can't retake my position and continue forward?

What the hell was it all for? All the sacrifice, the late nights, the unspeakable things I've done in the name of keeping my people safe?

I sit here on the borrowed bed and let myself mourn the life I've lost so suddenly. It's not until I feel the bed dip beside me do I realize he's come into the room.

I immediately shift to face away from him. Hell, all he needs is more ammunition to use against me. This is one more thing added to the list for him to mock me for. One more thing for him to poke and prod and punch.

"Go away. You don't have any reason to be in here."

His voice is soft when he answers, and I can feel his breath on the back of my neck. "You're crying."

That's all he says, like that's an answer to a question I didn't ask him.

I swipe my cheeks and sit up, throwing my chin up despite my no doubt puffy cheeks and red-rimmed eyes. "It's nothing to concern yourself with. I'm not physically hurt, just fucking weak."

He studies me, and I keep my eyes on him like he's about to go for my throat now that he knows I'm done.

Except. He doesn't.

He reaches out and wraps one solid around my shoulders and tugs me against his side. At first, I hesitate, but like last night, his grip is like iron, and I can't do anything to dislodge him. "It's not weak to cry. If it's something you need to do, then do it."

I swipe angrily as more tears fall. "Well, I don't need an audience for it. You've seen I'm fine. Now you can leave."

He tugs me tighter into him until I'm forced to melt myself against him or risk pulling my neck at the very least. My shoulders, too, at the most.

Since fighting seems to be useless, I let him hold me. It's awkward, especially as the memory of last night filters back and how very solid he felt against me. And he does now too. Like a boulder which can never be moved.

I sag into his chest and let the tears fall. It's too much now to hold them back. If he mocks me for it later, so be it. It'll give us something else to argue about.

After the tears stop and I can finally stop sobbing, I notice his fingers entwined in the hair at the nape of my neck, his other hand around my back holding me against him. I'm partially in his lap, partially on the bed, and he doesn't seem the least bit concerned about it.

But I sure as hell am. It's not taking comfort from him specifically, something I can't think about too hard, but the act of taking comfort in another person at all.

I gently ease away from him, and this time he lets me go. "Why would you do this? Hold me? You hate me."

His eyes are dark as he studies me, waiting for something...but I'm not sure what. "I never said I hate you."

"Well, you don't have to say it. Every time you call me princess, I can hear it in your tone. You don't know me, but you hate me. Why?"

"Again, I never said I hate you. There are parts of you I don't understand, that I don't like, but as a whole, I don't hate you."

I swallow, my throat suddenly thick. "You should go. I'm fine now."

"Are you sure? It's not weak to cry nor to take comfort in someone else. If it's something you need, then it's something you need."

I shake my head and turn away so he can't see the emotions chasing across my face. "A long time ago, I let myself believe I could have it all. Love, my people, everything. And fate showed me I was wrong. I can have power, or I can have love."

"So you chose power?"

I stay silent since we both already know the answer. "That sounds like a very lonely way to live your life."

This time, I face him, since I want to peel apart what he's thinking right now. "I'm not lonely. I have my people. I have...sex." I spare him the fact that I've had actual intercourse one time, and I didn't even finish. As far as he needs to know, I've learned all I need to. "There are people in my life. I'm not lonely."

His dark eyes stay locked on mine. "I don't believe you. You're a very good liar. The best I've met, in fact, besides myself. But you can't sell that lie. You're lonely. If it's so bad, why are you fighting for it? Why go back to that council if all you have there is an empty throne and an empty bed?"

I stiffen, and by the way his face resettles into his usual mask of arrogance, I know mine has slipped into place as well. "My bed is rarely empty. But that's absolutely no concern of yours. Thank you for the breakfast. Please let me know if you need me for anything else later."

He narrows his eyes, stands, and buttons his jacket. "There you go. That's the woman I don't understand. You'd rather push me away than let me see your vulnerability."

"Can you blame me when you've been a dick since we met?"

I want to know what he'll say, to see inside his head a moment, but he doesn't oblige. "Get some rest. It'll be another late night."

7

MICHAIL

She's obviously been affected by what happened more than I thought. I don't know why I was an idiot and thought she was fine. No, I do know why, because she acts like she's fine and the world isn't barreling toward a reckoning at any moment. She made me think she was fine, and because I didn't want to think too much about it, I didn't trust my gut.

Never again.

Everything in me is warring over her. To push her away and leave her alone like she says she wants or bring her in close, hold her tight, even as she fights against me.

I want to hate her. Despite my word. I want to hate her for everything she stands for, and for the world she lives in, this world she obviously knows nothing about. I want to hate her for things that aren't her fault, and I know it's not fair.

But life is never fair. I learned that at five, when I was sold for the first time. Life isn't fair, and the only way to get through it is to make sure you remember that little fact.

I grab my laptop out of my bag, strip my jacket off, and place it over a barstool at the small countertop. If I'm not spending my time hating her, then I need to get her out of my life as soon as possible. Complications aren't something I need right now. And Selena Aquila is one goddamned beautiful complication.

There's nothing new in my email from the Five, and nothing new from my contacts in Chicago. That doesn't mean there's not more to learn.

I swivel to dig my phone from my jacket pocket, hit the speed dial, and wait for Kai to answer.

"Hello?" His voice is sleep-rough and quiet.

"Wake up asshole. I have some work for you to do."

"Selena..."

Despite his outward disdain for his sister, that he asked about her first makes me think she doesn't know exactly how much Kai cares for her. A fun fact I'll save for later. "I want the reports on what happened to Selena. The reports on her attack. Anything you've got."

There's some shuffling through the phone, then I hear his fingers flying over the keyboard. "There's nothing much to go on. She didn't call the police, and the only reason it got reported at all was because the neighbors reported the noise complaint. Some of them reported gunshots."

Interesting. "Did she say anything to you when she called for help? Anything about killing her attackers? Or about who is trying to get to her?"

"No, but my sister isn't really a sharer. Not unless you want to start pulling out teeth to get the information."

I consider this little tidbit, but it makes sense. She doesn't trust anyone, Kai and me included, so why would she share her vulnerabilities when they can be used to harm her later? A sentiment I don't appreciate but understand.

"Just send me what you have. I'll see if I can get some answers out of her."

There's a long pause. Will he ask not to question her? But he doesn't. He whispers, "Good luck," and the phone goes dead.

I slide the phone next to my laptop and reach out to my Chicago contacts, but it will be awhile until they can come back with information, if they even have any. Seems pointless to carry on a useless search when I have the source of the information in the next room.

She might not be ready to talk, but I sure as hell am. The faster I get her safe and out of my life, the better.

I enter her room, and as usual, she cuts me a glare. "You really need to learn to knock. What if I was masturbating in here?"

I stop in the middle of the room, the image imprinting in my mind before I can stop it. Her beautiful long limbs splayed out, her tan skin glistening with sweat. I bite my bottom lip, working to keep my face neutral for the first time in a very long time. "Well, I guess I would have seen a lot more than I wanted to. But it wouldn't change the fact that I have questions and you need to answer them."

"Fine."

I've already got a speech prepared about why she needs to cooperate when I snap my mouth closed. "Fine?"

She tugs her blankets up to her waist, doing nothing to hide the soft swell of her breasts framed above the fabric. "Yes. Fine. It's the least I owe you for..."

A red tinge enters her cheeks, and I think back to earlier. "You don't owe me anything for that, but we need to go over the details of what happened to you, see if we can pinpoint the source and eradicate it quickly. We both agree the faster you are back in your world and me in mine, the better."

I sit on the edge of her bed, near her knees, and bring one leg up, my foot hanging over the side. "So tell me what you remember about that night?"

She blinks rapidly, dragging her eyes to her lap. "There was an event to open the season, as there always is, and I went home the same as usual. Nothing occurred at the party, not even a little bloodshed, so I thought maybe everything was fine in the society circles. Many were upset I offered to help Kai, instead of turning him over to your city's head councilwoman. I'd already called the detail up to start the next day since I knew he and Rose already had other security in place."

I wave her on. "I don't care about that. Get to the part where you realized you were in trouble."

Her voice wavers. "My alarm didn't go off. I remember it clearly. I woke up, the house silent, and yet, I just felt like I wasn't alone."

"And then..."

She keeps her eyes on her lap. Maybe to protect herself, or maybe so I can't read things she doesn't want me to see in her eyes. "I grabbed the gun I keep under the pillow, and the second I felt the air stir around the bed, I fired the first shot. I must have hit someone, because I heard them go down and then someone grabbed me around the throat. I put the gun against his head, and I fired again. I don't think he expected me to react that way while he was choking me."

Carefully, she curves her fingers around her neck, again, as if protecting it. There's a faint purple smudge there I hadn't noticed. Or maybe she covered it up with makeup.

I shift on the bed and gently peel her fingers away. "Is this a bruise?" A purple necklace rings her neck, and I'm ashamed of myself for not having noticed. I spent so much time trying not to look at her, that I missed something vital.

I jerk the covers off her lap and look at her legs. There are bruises on her knees, one on her thigh almost near the hem of her shorts. "Are there anymore? What else are you hiding?"

She flinches at my tone, and I curse myself. "I apologize. I didn't mean to make it sound like your fault, but I need to know what they did to you. Exactly. Did they..." I glance at her skinned knees.

"No, this was when I stumbled over the side of the bed and landed on my knees instead of my feet. I was just trying to get out from under the guy who grabbed me, so I didn't think. There were others waiting, but I had a bag for emergencies in the closet and an escape route. I hid there, dressed, and snuck through the tunnel hatch to exit the garage and ran into the small patch of woods behind my house."

I nod, encouraging her. "You were smart to have a backup plan. Did you see anything else? Anyone you recognized, any vehicles?"

She toys with the hem of her tank top, then slowly lifts it to reveal a large bruise across one side of her ribs. It looks like it's healing, but there's no way to know if her ribs broke too. "Did you get that looked at?"

"Yes, my sister knows a doctor. He checked everything out, said I was fine."

I open a note on my phone. "What's his name? I'll want to speak to him."

"He didn't have anything to do with it. Neither did my sister."

I sigh. "That's not what I asked. I'm just trying to get the details. This will be easier with all the facts."

She shakes her head. "He helped me. I'll tell you everything I know, but I won't risk him or my sister in this."

"Where is your sister?" I hadn't thought about asking Kai or her if they knew she was safe.

This time, she shrugs with a rueful smile. "If I know my younger sister Julia, and I certainly do, she's probably working her own angles to figure out what happened to me.

Julia…Julia…where do I know that name? It hits me. "Your sister is Julia Aquila?" Why hadn't I put that together before, about Selena, or Kai for that matter? Holy shit. One of the few most respected and well-known members of society, Julia Aquila's reputation as an assassin who can't be bribed precedes her.

"As I said, I want to keep her out of this, at least as much as she'll allow me to."

I'm still a little dumb struck, so I simply nod. "Did you get any threats at the season opening party? Or anything before then? Or any offers of alliance you turned down that might have angered anyone?"

She shakes her head. "Only that bitch of a head councilwoman, and the man you met at my house the other night. Do you think she orchestrated things? Put all this in motion to stir the board while she went for Kai?"

It's a possibility I have to consider. If Selena isn't in danger anymore, then we'll know soon enough. But for now, we operate as if she's still at risk.

She pulls the covers over her lap again, hiding her bruises, and all her tan bare skin. "Any other questions?"

My mind shifts back to the councilmember who showed up at her house. "Had you met that man before?"

She shakes her head. "No, never. Why?"

"Maybe he knows something that can help. I don't suggest offering an alliance, but at the very least, we might be able to make friends and see what he can do for us." More than he already has.

I think he's the councilmember Andrea has been shadowing, but if that's the case, then he's the one who had something to do with her attack. If what he is doing now is an attempt to make up for his actions, it won't work. Alliance or not, I'll slit his throat and toss him in the river. I don't care how many ways he helps us.

"What are you thinking about? You just got a particularly savage look on your face, and I'm not sure if I should be scared or worried for someone else."

I lick my lips and give her a little grin. One that makes her eyes go wide as she takes in my face. I've known what I look like since I was a teenager. I used to hate it, but now, I've learned to use my looks to my advantage. "Not scared, no. But I think we should call this councilman and agree to a meeting. See if he can offer us anything useful."

She swallows, loud enough for me to hear. "Useful?"

I shrug and stand, done with my questions for now. "Yes, but this time you can skip the dress. We'll meet him privately. We want him to know who you are."

There's something almost feral in her eyes as she gazes up at me. "And who am I to be for this meeting?"

I head toward the door and call back, "A queen."

8

SELENA

I don't know if what we have can be called a truce. What he did for me, the comfort he offered, created a momentary ceasefire, nothing more.

At least that's what I tell myself as I nibble on a salad while watching him read something on his tablet. I tell myself I'm looking for reasons to hate him, reasons to get away and take care of myself, reasons to treat him like every other man who's come before.

Yet, I can't exactly deny I'm also looking for that smile he gave me. The tiniest one turned his whole broodingly beautiful face into something a painter would immortalize. I didn't even know men could be so...

He shifts in the seat, never taking his eyes off the tablet. "You're staring awfully hard right now."

I swallow the bite of salad I'd stopped chewing. "How do you even know? You're reading."

"I can feel it."

I roll my eyes even though he's not looking at me. "You can't feel when someone stares at you. That's not a scientifically proven thing."

"Actually..." He pauses to sip his coffee. "There is a very specific part of the brain that's only job is to notice where others are looking. It can be developed, over time, like a sixth sense. Some brain cells only activate when someone is looking at you."

Quietly, I close my flopped open mouth and stare down at my picked over salad. My face is burning, not from his correction, but that I sat here staring at him for a good five minutes, and he knew the entire time.

Shit. I need to change the subject or risk embarrassing myself further. "Is there anything we need to do today?"

He still doesn't look over at me. "I've got several weapons that need cleaning if you find yourself bored."

"Not bored enough for that."

"Well, probably a little too lowbrow for the likes of you anyway. Who has time to clean their own weapons?"

I grit my teeth and stab my fork into my salad. I've been doing my best to keep my mouth shut and not push his buttons. He has zero qualms about walking into a room and rolling all over mine. In fact, he seems to delight in riling me until I want to find one of these weapons and shoot him with his own guns.

Barely, I keep myself in line and don't respond to his pokes. "How about some books?"

He waves his mug toward a shelf near the far wall. Why does he have a bookshelf in a hotel room? Does he live here, or did he bring those in when we arrived, or before? I hadn't noticed it until now, but then again, I spend most of my time in the room he gave me. Not like he wants me around anyway.

"Why are your books in this hotel room?"

Now he finally looks up, his eyes narrowing as he locks on mine. A tendril of his hair falls over one eye, but he doesn't seem to notice. "Get some rest. Read if you like, but we'll have a late meeting tonight. The councilman you met has finally agreed to meet us and discuss terms."

I slosh lettuce around the bowl. "Terms?"

"He seems to think you want to make an alliance with him. We'll have to set him straight that we only want information tonight. We don't know enough about him to ensure he won't betray us at the first opportunity."

"But he helped save Kai? Isn't that what you said, or he did, the night we met?"

He shrugs, turning back to his tablet. "One good deed doesn't rectify a lifetime of brutality."

"So what do we..."

Michail stands abruptly, pulls his vibrating cell phone from his pocket, and walks out of the room without another word.

I definitely still hate this self-righteous asshole. Instead of finishing the salad I have no interest in, I abandon it on the table, grab a book from the shelf, and retreat to my room. He can finish his lunch alone for all I care. From now on, too, if we are going to have such scintillating conversations over our meals. I won't bother if he's not trying.

I settle in my bed with the book I grabbed. It doesn't even matter what the title is. I'm bored out of my ever-loving mind and hate that I'm stuck sitting here and not out there taking back my territory. There has to be more I can do than lie around reading. Staying alive is important, but I don't think I can handle staying alive to go back to nothing when this is all over.

They want me to give in. Surrender. And if I send word, I'll back down and give up my seat on the council, they'll probably stop coming for me. But I can't do it. Not when they took it, not when they stole everything and expected to get away with what's mine.

His voice interrupts the dark spiral of my thoughts. "I said you could borrow that book, not destroy it."

I stare down at the way I'm clutching the book open, the spine bowed unnaturally. 'My apologies. If I've ruined it, I'll buy you another copy."

His eyes narrow, and he crosses to sit on my bed. The man walks in without a knock and throws himself on my bed like he owns it, or like he's been invited, and I sure as shit didn't give him permission.

Maybe I'm just being irritable. Letting my emotions get to me. "What do you want? You walked away from the table without a word. I assumed that was your half-assed version of a dismissal."

He shifts so he can look at me, his full lips drawn down as they usually are. "I'll leave that one alone in the interest of saving time. We need to discuss a few things before the meeting tonight."

I slap the book closed and set it beside me on the bed. "I'm not an idiot. I've been negotiating with people like this man for years. It's what my parents trained me to do. Kai learned computers and guns. Julia learned knives and secrets. I learned people and power."

His gaze roves my face and down my body, then back up. "You can't defend yourself at all?"

"I didn't say that. How do you think I got away after the initial attack? Between Kai and Julia, I learned what I needed to keep myself alive in the viper's den of politics. They made sure I'd be able to handle myself if the need arose. Apparently our world has gotten darker, grittier, since my parents' day. They didn't think I needed such things."

He huffs, or snorts. I can't tell. "It wasn't any less dark or gritty then, it was just more secretive. The crimes were hidden; the evil deeds tucked away so no one could see."

I glance at his arm, below the rolled-up sleeve of his white button-down shirt. "Many crimes are still hidden away."

"I didn't come here to talk about any of this. What we need to discuss is how to get the councilman to give us what we need without you giving him anything in return."

I open my mouth with a retort, but he walks out of the room. This time I surge out of the bedding, ready to go after him, but I don't get to the door before he's back, a garment bag in hand. "This is for tonight."

"Why do you keep giving me clothing? I have very nice, very

expensive clothing of my own. Besides, this is probably not even my" —I unzip the bag and spread it open—"style," I finish in a whisper.

He's hovering, his hands shoved into his slacks pockets. "If you can't use it, you are welcome to find something local to wear, and I'll have it delivered, but it won't be tailored."

I'm speechless staring at the rose-gold bandage dress. It's stunning and will give me far more attention than either of us wants on me right now. "Are you sure about this? People will look."

"You have a high opinion of yourself."

I pull the dress out of the bag and resist petting the smooth fabric. "No, I just know what I look like. It's a skill the same as anything else. I look the way I do, and maintain my look, so I can use it to my advantage."

When I lay the dress on the bed, I spot the shoes in the bag's bottom. They are equally stunning, and just as expensive as the dress. "I can pay for these things myself. I don't want to inconvenience you."

He shifts beside me, surprising me with how close he is. "I don't need your money, Princess. I can afford anything I need to buy." His words are stinging, but his tone isn't meant to cut like it had been before.

Even though he's a hard-ass, the ceasefire stands for him too.

But how long until one of us breaks it and fires the first shot?

I clear my throat, stepping back, praying I don't look like I'm retreating. The scent of his soap, or cologne, lemongrass and something spicy, is close and cloying and doing things in my belly. "Well, thank you. I'll be ready when it's time to go down."

He gives me a long assessing look, like he's trying to fit the last few puzzle pieces in place, and they just don't seem to work. "Fine, be ready at ten, and we'll go down."

Once he leaves, I scramble into the bathroom and hope I have everything I need to get ready properly. At ten sharp, I walk out of the bedroom wearing the dress I would have bought for myself, but it seems so much heavier with him buying it and him staring at me wearing it with his haunted eyes.

We go down to the casino floor, but immediately head into a side door into an underground tunnel. It's deserted, and I try to keep up with his long pace in my obscenely high heels. Once we get to another row of doors, we slip into one and are met by a man who looks like he could be security, or a waiter. I can't tell since it's dark, and the man is in all black.

We are led into a small dining room set with a table for four.

Candlelight glitters off the chandelier, and Michail shifts behind me. I'm about to turn when he gently eases me toward the table by the elbow and pulls out the chair. "Sit, relax. We have a few minutes. We are early."

I sit, and he grabs my hand, bringing it to his lips and kissing the back.

"What the fuck?" I try to jerk away, but his eyes blaze, locking on mine.

"Like the other night when we each played a role, tonight too, we both have a part to play. You, the queen, and me, the besotted lover. Your protection and your conquest."

His lips skim my knuckles, and I try to relax with him holding my hand that way. He takes the seat beside mine and drags my hand, still attached to his, into his lap.

I don't have time to think of some argument against this because the door on the other end of the room is thrown open and a stunning woman saunters in. She's dressed in all black with blood-red nails, black stilettos, and her long, dark hair hangs in a smooth sheet to her hips. The councilman I'd already met walks in next, and they both assess us, then sit across from us at the table.

I stare at the woman and man, and shake myself into the task at hand. Get the information we need and give nothing in return.

When I shift to extend my hand to the woman, she beats me there. "Andrea," she says, her voice smoke and shadows. No doubt every man's fantasy. She gives Michail a familiar nod, and I glance at him. He knows her.

I focus on the councilman. He's older than his date, but his face is perfectly symmetrical, his eyes shining and strangely kind despite his position. No one on any council could ever be called kind. "I didn't introduce myself when we met before. You may call me Emmanuelle."

"Selena."

A waiter enters, pours everyone a glass of white wine and retreats again. Michail squeezes my hand and teases his fingers up my wrist to the joint in my elbow, as if he's nothing more than window dressing.

I glance between the two of them, unsure how to begin.

The councilman jumps right in before I can open my mouth. "I'm here to renew my offer of an alliance."

He pulls something out of his pocket. Michail tenses beside me, but relaxes when it's just a box. But I don't relax, not because it's not a weapon, but because there's only one thing he could offer with that little velvet box.

Gently, he pries open the lid, revealing a massive rose cut diamond. "Ms. Aquilla, I'd like to ask for your hand in marriage."

9

MICHAIL

She's obviously going to tell the crazy man, "No, thank you," and then approach the topic of information.

I wait.

And wait. The room is so quiet despite the roil of sound I know lies outside the doors to the main casino floor. I risk a quick flick of my eyes at Andrea, who is staring down at the ring with the same slack-jawed expression Selena is wearing. If I knew diamonds shut women up so thoroughly, I might have tried to use them sooner.

Selena breaks the silence. "Why would you want to marry me?"

Emmanuelle leans toward her, a small smile playing on his lips. "If we allied, our two big cities combined in power would be unstoppable."

She shakes her head, squeezing my hand without realizing it. "No, I mean, why would you want to marry me, especially right now? I have nothing to offer you. At the moment, the security guy at the door holds a higher position of power than I do."

I'm about to cut in, change the subject, something. This isn't what we discussed. She's supposed to be playing up her place in the world at the moment. It's the whole damn reason I'm sitting here playing the besotted pup.

"I have every confidence you'll regain your seat of power and eradicate any resistance."

Selena smiles at him, her white teeth flashing against her bright red lips. "I'm glad one of us is feeling confident tonight. So, help me out. Sweeten the deal for me."

He gives her the regal nod these assholes must have to practice in the mirror. "What would you like?"

I tense at her bitter tone. "Tell me who I need to hunt down and eradicate so I can take back my city."

It's on the tip of my tongue to jerk her back against me, scream at him to get the hell out. Anything to acknowledge the fact that the ring is still glinting in the candlelight, and she hasn't told him no yet.

"I'm afraid I don't have that information. Like many, I assumed my former head councilwoman had orchestrated a diversion so she could capture your brother with little fanfare. Now that her schemes have been revealed, it seems there was something deeper at work in your territory. Someone unhappy with the power dynamics looking for the first opportunity to strike. The councilwoman gave it to them."

She leans in, riveted to his every word. Something sharp twists in my gut. "But you don't know who it is? What they want?"

The other man shakes his head mournfully and glances to Andrea at his side. They share a long look, one I don't understand, and I'm very good at reading people.

Selena settles back into her seat, and then jolts, staring down at where she's dragged our joined hands into her lap. "Sorry," she whispers.

I give her a little shake of my head. Not while he's here. Right now, I'm still playing the part, and so is she.

I think she understands when her spine snaps straight and she eyes Emmanuelle and Andrea. "I'd like to consider this offer."

The man reaches out and snaps the ring box closed. "You can have forty-eight hours, and then I'll go with plan B."

I'm pretty sure I don't want to know what plan B is, and neither does Selena.

"Please understand, councilman, I was the head of my own city. Marrying you, becoming your wife, would be a step down, in my opinion."

He leans forward, his face going red, but Selena holds up her hand to finish. "Not because of you personally, of course, but because I know how our world works. A woman alone might be considered powerful, if she can back her power up, but a woman married is only an extension of her husband. I can't give up that kind of power, not easily. Not without careful consideration."

Andrea is leaning on his arm, whispering into his ear. I catch the exchange from under the fall of my curls, studying Andrea. Of course, she is here on orders from Kai, or Adrian, but I'm very curious to know what she's supposed to be doing, and why it's with this particular councilmember. One who's crossed our path a lot lately. Something to ask Kai when I check in next.

Emmanuelle claps his hand on the sides of his chair and shoves to stand. "Well, I see no point in lingering. You may consider and let me know your answer."

His eyes shift to me and narrow before he turns and holds his arm out for Andrea to take. There's a heartbeat of hesitation she covers up as she grasps his arm and leans in close, her hips swaying against his as they walk out of the glittering dining room.

I release my hold on Selena and sit back. "Why is it when you powerful people meet up, no one actually eats or drinks anything? Hell, no one even got to order."

She snorts once, then laughs loud, bending over to laugh more, hiding her mouth behind her hands. When she comes back to herself, her eyes rimmed in tears, she shakes her head. "I have no idea. I suspect it started because people didn't want to be poisoned, but now, I don't know."

As much as I want to share her laughter, I can't. She might look normal, laughing in her couture, but she's just like the rest of them. People who buy and sell others, moving them around like pieces on a game board.

"Let's go," I say, standing. I extend my hand to help her to her feet.

We take the back exit again and grab the first elevator. It's not until we are halfway to our suite do I notice she's shivering. One quick glance tells me she's physically fine, and she's not crying. "Are you alright?"

Her eyes are locked on the numbers, and she sways slightly on her feet. Enough that I wrap my arm around her middle and hold her tightly to my side until we reach our floor. It takes seconds to swing her into my arms and walk her into our suite. I march straight for my bed, the first thing coming to mind.

Her eyes are fluttering open and closed. It's not until I lie her on top of the covers that she relaxes and stops shivering. Did I miss something? Was she injured and hid it from me? There's no way I wouldn't have seen something in the figure hugging cut of this dress, or the tiny shorts she's always wandering around the suite in.

I tap her cheek gently, trying to wake her, but she doesn't stir. So, I go for plan B and make her as comfortable as possible. Gently, I remove her shoes, massaging up her calf muscles, then pull a blanket from the end of the bed to cover her with.

Still nothing.

Shit. I try to tap her cheek again. "Selena, wake up. If you die on me, your brother will kill me, and this will all have been a colossal waste. Wake up."

She stirs, and I let out a sigh, relaxing, remembering I'm wearing this fucking costume still. I strip off my jacket, the tie, open all the buttons at the collar and sleeves, trying to give myself room to breathe.

Slowly, she blinks her eyes open, staring at the ceiling. Then she drops her gaze and pins me with her eyes. "What the hell happened?"

"You tell me. We were in the elevator, and you just passed out. I had to carry you in here."

She stares around and touches the blanket at her waist. "Where is here?"

"My bed, in our suite."

"Why did you bring me to your bed, and not my own? It's closer to the door."

For fuck's sake. I sit beside her legs, shoving them over to make more room. "You're really arguing with me right now when you're the one who passed out? I took you straight here because it was my first thought."

Her eyes narrow. "That you'd want me in your bed, or that I'd want to be in your bed?"

"Stop twisting my goddamn words. You being in my bed means nothing. I was just trying to assess if you were injured."

She sits up and groans. "I'm fine. Thank you."

I want to punch a hole through the fucking wall. "You're fine," I say, deadpan. Then yell, "You're fine?"

She stares at me, her eyes narrowing again. "Do not speak to me like that."

"You are not fine. Not if you are even entertaining the idea of marrying that guy. Why didn't you stick to the plan? Why didn't you just tell him no right there at the table?"

She drops her shoulder and sits higher, straighter, like a queen commanding attention. And when her cleavage pushes at the edge of her dress like that, yeah, I'm paying attention, whether or not I want to. "What does it matter to you? If this is how I get out of this fucking hotel room and back to my life, then maybe I should consider it."

"I didn't do all of this, and keep you safe, so you can just sell yourself away for nothing. You don't even know if he's capable of protecting you. He gave you absolutely no assurances."

"Marriages have been forged with less, I assure you. If I must trade what dregs of my power are left for freedom, for protection, then it's what I have to do."

I narrow my eyes. "Who says? You can protect yourself. I'm here, right now, under orders from your brother to protect you. This marriage isn't even an option. It's a distraction."

She stands, her tone sharpening, her eyes turning cold. "You don't know shit about selling yourself for the promise of protection. You don't know anything about what it feels like to be considered the least important person in a room. The one everyone else uses, abuses, and discards. That's what it's like to be a woman in our society. That is what I've been working to change. If that means I have to do it as a wife instead of a queen, so be it."

I stand, stunned, my anger bubbling under my skin like a professional swimmer's trail, never breaking the surface, only setting it roiling. "Are you fucking kidding me?"

It's dumb, but I can't help but react around her. She does something to my self-control I can't repair. I rip open my shirt and jerk it off my arms to toss to the ground. Then I turn so she can see my back. Or rather, the mess of my back when Sal's family's buyers got finished with me. "Don't you dare tell me I don't know what it feels like to be used or abused. You think these scars were voluntary? No. This happens when a beautiful child is sold by a sadist to a pedophile. I've been violated in more ways than you can ever even know is possible."

I face her again and grab her chin in my hand, hard. There are tears swimming in her eyes, and I curl my lip at the sight of them. "I don't want your fucking pity."

One tear slips down her cheek. "I don't pity you."

I swipe the tear away and settle both hands on her warm cheeks, using my thumbs to bat each tear as it falls. My anger fizzles away like the death of a sparkler, shining brightly, telling me to crush her here and now, and then it's gone, dead with the softness in her eyes. "Then what is this, if not pity?"

Her forehead knots and she searches my eyes, sliding her gaze back and forth between mine. "It's sadness. I'm sad about what you went through, and sad that I haven't been able to change the world enough yet to spare the next child put in that position."

It's not a reaction, but a necessity. I don't think as I settle my mouth over hers and brush our lips together.

10

SELENA

I'm not sure how he went from spitting curses at me to kissing me. It's thrilling and terrifying at the same time, not knowing who he'll be today. The man who hates me, or the one trying to unlock my secrets. Or maybe the one with the haunted wild eyes waiting for me in the dark. I can't know, and that's part of the draw.

And I am drawn to him. Even as much as I think I hate him.

I settle my hands on his chest and stay still while he rubs his lips over mine. It's more of an exploration than a kiss, but I still feel it in every part of my body. My toes are tingling and there's already a soft gentle pulse in my clit matching the erratic beat of my heart. He tastes cool, like clean ice-cold water, and fuck, I want to drown in him.

But I can't.

I gently push his chest, enough that he gets the message and stops kissing me. Except he doesn't stop kissing me, but simply opens his eyes, his mouth still sliding along mine. If he won't stop, then I'll have to be the strong one here.

I ease away from him, and the more distance I get, the easier it is to get more distance. I race out of the room, back to my room, and slam the door hard enough to rattle the pictures on the walls.

Fuck. Shit. His kissing me changed something. It wasn't even a real kiss. Nothing more than a six grader might try as a first attempt on the playground. Nothing but his lips on mine.

It might be a convincing lie if I didn't feel it still in every part of me.

Damn. I need a drink, and I'm not about to go out there rooting around for one. Not if he's going to be there looking all...

I shake my head, find some shoes since I left mine in his room apparently, and grab a few twenties from my suitcase. Quietly, I creak open the door to check for his presence. He's not there and his door is closed, so I creep out, gently ease the heavy room door open and sneak into the hallway.

When I reach the elevator without him barreling after me, I let out a long sigh. It only takes a few minutes to get to the ground floor and the waiting bar nearest the elevator. It's styled after an old pub, and I don't even care as I signal the bartender for an old-fashioned.

I settle on the stool farthest from the door and cup the drink closer. At the very least, it will dull some of this ache which seems to have awakened inside me over nothing, absolutely nothing. "It was barely a kiss," I mumble into my glass, and take a long gulp, letting the alcohol burn its way down my throat.

I manage to finish my drink and order another before he finds me, storming into the pub, causing many of the patrons to take one look at him and run.

With a little buzz bravery, I swivel on the stool and pat the one next to me. "Join me, please. You could probably use one of these yourself."

His chest is heaving, his eyes dark, his curls shoved away from his face like he's been spearing his fingers through them. "Do you have any idea what..." He stops and takes a long inhale through his nose and then out through his mouth. "You are a bigger brat than I thought. Coming down here, putting yourself at risk, for what, a damn drink? Was it worth it? Is that drink right there"—he points to my almost empty second glass— "worth taking a bullet to the head?"

He brings his fingers up and presses them to my temple. "That is how quick and easy someone could take you out. You're practically doing their job for them right now."

I swallow the rest of the liquid, letting it turn more of the sharp thoughts in my brain to soft mushy balls that I can't quite pick up. This is better. Before, I felt everything. Now, it's all a gentle haze.

I throw money on the bar and stand, swaying on my feet. He lets out a colorful curse and turns away from me, no doubt trying to calm himself by the tension across his shoulders.

Looking at him, his shirt open at the neck and loose, I can still see the cuts in his skin, the perfectly straight lines on his back like someone was keeping time in flesh and blood. Each little tick a countdown to what? I'm not brave enough to ask him, not right now.

"We can go back up if you want?" I say, trying to appease him a little at least.

He spins to face me again, and his eyes are hot now, raging. "We can go back up if I want? Really, how kind of you, *Princess*. But first, we are taking a little field trip."

Not so gently, he locks his hand around my wrist and drags me out of the bar, onto the main floor, and down the back entrance we used earlier into the tunnels. They lead to a big concrete central room, which then extends off to multiple hallways. Except, we stop at the hub, and he flips the lights on. It's still dark and shadowy, barely enough light illuminating the center.

He waves his hand. "You see this pit?"

I nod, wondering if he means something else, trying to grasp the nuance of whatever lesson he's trying to impart, if only so we can go back upstairs sooner. I shiver and wrap my arms around myself.

"This is where so many of our enemies have been taken out. The walls here don't echo, even if you think they should. The sound of a bullet doesn't carry."

I'm still trying to understand what he's saying, but not saying. "Is this your way of telling me you're done babysitting and intend to kill me yourself?"

He jerks my arm and drags me into an adjacent room, flips the light, and slams the door. Then he picks me up around the waist as if I weigh nothing and sits me on the desk. "This is my way of telling you how easy it is to take care of a problem when there are no more solutions to it."

He steps into me, and for some reason, I widen my legs to let him get close. It's dumb, and I can't explain it except part of me wants that cool clear taste of him again. One more time, like this, when it won't be so strong. When it won't come with freezing burn.

I'm not brave enough to reach for him first, so we stare at each other, him taller, me having to crane my neck to look up into his eyes.

"You're a fucking idiot," he whispers. "Do you know how quickly you could have been gone?"

I nod, not because I feel bad about getting a drink, because it's the answer he wants. Of course, I understand I put myself at risk, but he seems to think I'm more fragile than I actually am. "What now?"

Isn't that the question?

He slides his hands up my bare arms so gently, it almost feels like a ghost passing, a lingering touch long enough to send goosebumps across my flesh and nothing more. He stops when he settles his hands on my cheeks again. "You're a goddamned fucking brat."

I gulp as he tilts my face again. This time, I know it's coming. His mouth slants over mine, and this kiss is nothing like the first.

He takes my mouth with the same intensity he spits curses or screams at me. As if he can devour me whole from the inside out. And maybe I want him to.

His teeth scrape along mine, his tongue lays siege, and every part of my mouth becomes his. He marks me, scrapes me, licks me, sucks me, and all I can do is hold on to him and whimper.

The second he releases me, I suck in a great gasp of a breath and stare up at him. He tenses, the tendons in his neck going taut, his chest heaving, as his scars peek above the open buttons. "Why am I doing this?"

I shake my head, unable to speak. Fuck if I know.

He licks his lips, testing, tasting me there. His eyes are bright, his muscles tense, but he still holds my face so gently. "I don't know what's going on here."

This time, I find my voice, enough to goad him. "It's called lust. You might know that if you weren't a virgin."

He narrows his eyes, releases my face, and grabs the hem of my dress. For a second, I think he's going to rip it and I screech, trying to grab his hands, but he jerks it up around my hips, exposing my inner thighs, my scrap of lace panties.

"A virgin, huh?" he says.

I risk his wrath and nod, unsure of where this is going. What he doesn't need to know is that I'm also a virgin. I definitely don't have any experience. Not with kissing, or with any of it. Hell, I haven't even had a proper orgasm before. So I can't mock him. Not that I volunteer any of this information.

He puts his hand over my pussy. Straight grabs me, his fingers toward my opening and his wrist toward my clit. "For a virgin, I seem to have at least gotten you all hot and bothered."

I sputter with my words. "It's not like that?"

"Not like what?" He dips his fingers into the edge of my panties, sliding along the wetness there, and he's right. I'm so fucking wet, even my thighs are slippery from it.

He pulls his fingers away from my skin and slides them into his mouth. It's obscene, and fucking hell if my entire body doesn't throb in time with my clit at the action. He sucks his fingers off and wraps both hands around my thighs. "Seems pretty obvious to me that if I dropped to my knees right here and buried my face in that pretty little cunt, you'd scream for me. You'd writhe against my face and ride my tongue until you came hard enough to see stars."

I gulp. It's not something I've ever imagined, but now that he's said the words, the image is in my head, and it's enough to make it harder to breathe. I'm almost shaking and sick with the need for him to touch me.

He doesn't though. He stands there, my knees against his thighs, his wet fingers so close to where I want them and yet so far away. "Admit it?"

"What?" I whisper, then clear my throat. "Admit what?"

He leans in so his mouth is almost against mine. "Admit that you'd let me fuck you right now. Admit that me kissing you got you so turned on, you ran to find an outlet that wasn't riding my cock."

His words are obscene, and I want to deny them, but I can't. Not when the evidence is there for him to test himself, and he is more than willing to call my bluff on that side of things.

My throat is dry, the alcohol swimming heavy in my gut. "What do you want me to say?"

He leans in, and I tense, thinking he means to kiss me. Instead, he runs his nose down my jaw to my neck, then his eyes lock on my cleavage, and he stills, staring at the swell. "Simply admit you want me right now, and we'll call it even."

"But why?"

His breath is warm against my tits, and my nipples get hard. "Call it an act of faith. You admit I have some power over you, even if it's this tiny thing. I'll consider it a concession, and we can all get some sleep."

I swallow again, my voice not working right. Fuck. When he puts it like that, I don't want to say shit, but I don't know what fresh torture he might inflict on me next. Or if I'll have the will to resist.

"Fine." I shove at his chest, letting the anger sink in, even if it doesn't nearly match the lust. "I want you, okay? Is that enough to appease your ego, or do you need more?"

The corner of his lip lifts, and I swear he almost looks sad. "It's enough. Now, let's get you upstairs."

He steps back enough for me to slide off the desk, my stomach hitting the floor along with my feet, but then he's back, pressing all along my body, and in my face. "But test me again, Selena, and I swear I'll fuck you so hard, you won't have a single ounce of your own free will left. If that's the only way to keep you under control, I'm not above it. So, don't push it."

11

MICHAIL

I don't regret touching her, but I sure as hell will if Kai hears about it. I'm not afraid of him, but I also respect him too much to go against his wishes. No matter how much I want to peel Selena out of her clothing and see how much I can take her apart with my mouth.

It might be cowardly, but the next morning, I am the one doing the hiding. Not that she is seeking my company on a regular basis anyway.

At the same time, we will have to butt heads soon enough when we discuss the dismissal of Emmanuelle's proposal. Which reminds me.

I pull out my phone, hit Andrea on my speed dial, and wait while it rings.

I'm almost ready to hang up when she answers with a rough, "Hello?"

"You had to know I'd be calling as soon as I was able. What the hell was last night about? Why were you even there? And dare I ask what your interest in our councilman is?"

There's some shuffling through the line and she sighs. "You woke me up to grill me? Do you know how hard it's been for me to sleep since..."

Neither of us finishes that sentence.

"I'm sorry," I say, "but I need answers, and you are uniquely situated to give them to me. What the hell is going on between you and him?"

"You aren't my boss, so you don't get to make demands of me. But, since you annoy me the least of all you assholes, I'll just say it's a perpetual game of cat and mouse."

Shit. Does Kai know about this? Adrian? "Did you run it by the man who can actually give you orders?"

She lets out a long list of colorful curses. "Who the fuck do you think put me at his side? I don't have a choice. If I did, his head would be a decoration for my bedroom right now."

Andrea doesn't usually feel strongly about society members one way or the other unless they wrong her, which means Emmanuelle somehow ended up on her shit list. Something tells me that asking for specifics won't work.

"Fine, tell me why he wants to marry Selena. Do you know what kind of shit fit Kai would throw if he found out she was even considering it?"

She snorts, her voice low and soft. "I can only imagine having that asshole at Christmas dinner every year. Although from what I hear, Selena is a handful all on her own."

The urge to defend her rises, but I ignore it, thankful I've had a long time to practice staying mindful of my reactions. "Well, for right now, she's our responsibility. And I can't let her trade one form of danger for another in a prettier package."

"You think you'll have any luck convincing her either way? If so, you know even less about women than I thought."

It's my turn to sigh, and along with that little nugget, hang up on her.

Selena might not listen when I speak, but she sure as hell melted into my arms last night. For the first time, the fight in her eyes dimmed enough for reason to break through. I'm just not sure it's a great idea for either of us to use intimacy as a way to keep her in line, if it would even work outside of her being slightly buzzed from her free roam around the bar.

I don't get the proper time to consider, because she emerges from her room looking freshly rumpled, her hair in a messy bun, the long bare line of her leg distracting me.

"You finally came out of your room," she says, as she throws herself in the chair across from the table with a yawn.

I don't like her insinuating I was hiding, but I let it go. "Because we need to figure out what you are going to do."

She waves her hand between us. "There is no we in this situation. You're not the one marrying that asshole, so this is strictly a *me* decision."

"What do you think Kai would say if he heard about this?"

The look she gives me might have scared me if I hadn't been on the receiving end of Kai's very same look. "My brother has zero say in my life. Me asking for help was a fluke that he has taken full advantage of by appointing you my babysitter. I am not likely to be calling him for help again soon."

Throwing her over the edge of the table and using her smart mouth for something far better than spouting off sounds so good, but it won't help when I need her to tell me what is going on in her power-addled mind right now. "I neither agree nor disagree about it being your decision. But I think you need to weigh your choices and advantages."

"I'm already working on that." She grabs a piece of pizza from the box I left in the middle of the table. "I'm not about to offer myself up to be used and thrown away the second he gets what he wants."

"That's what I mean. You don't know what he really wants. He says an alliance, but we need to do more research to figure out if he has ulterior motives."

She rolls her eyes, swallowing a bite of pizza. "You think I'm an idiot? I didn't rise to govern my city by believing every pretty lie that spews from a man's mouth. In fact, I consider most of what men say to be lies, until I prove otherwise."

"That must be inconvenient."

She leans forward on her elbows, nothing but fire in her eyes. "For example, you threatening to screw me into submission is definitely a lie. We've, or rather, I've established you're a virgin, so I doubt you'll be capable of such a feat."

There's a self-satisfied little grin on her face as she studies me, as if she thinks her taunts are enough to get me to what...ravish her to prove my prowess? Or drive me into a rage? Maybe that's how the men in her life usually react, and even if she is capable of sending my brain into overdrive, I still like to consider my actions before I make a move.

For example, when I shove off the table and stand, then go around to her side and kneel next to her chair, I've already gone through all the ways I could make her scream my name.

When I turn her chair to face me in one quick jerk, I've already imagined shoving her thighs apart and burying my face in her sweet little cunt.

I do none of those things. I let her stare down her nose at me, waiting, watching while her breathing grows shallower, her hands clench on the edge of the chair. Every heartbeat I keep her in suspense, she winds herself up all on her own. It's a tactic I've used hundreds of times during my very thorough interrogations. This is entirely different though. I didn't expect how much it would affect me. My cock is already hard from my imagination.

I need to proceed before I do something we'll both regret. Something I haven't considered.

"And what are the benefits of marrying him?" I ask.

Her eyes slash up to mine from where she'd been scanning down my kneeling body. "Well, protection. Your council has a much more robust security force."

I balance on the balls of my feet and run my fingers up the back of her bare, muscular calf. "That would be our fault. The council fears the Five. They think more security will keep them safe."

"And will it?"

I stop at the sexy curve at the back of her knee. "No, we won't take the council down by force. By the time we finish with them, they will beg us to let them move on with their lives. They'll be begging us to let them run."

She shivers under my fingertips, trembling with each pass of my fingers. "So why get involved? If you plan to take your revenge anyway, why do you care what I choose to do?"

"Probably because I know what it's like to sell yourself in exchange for safety. Even if the deal is good, I don't want to see anyone have to face that decision."

I keep my eyes on her leg and continue traveling my fingers up to her thigh, curving my hand around the outside. It would be easier to say I'm touching her for a reason, a reason other than I want to feel how soft her skin is. For now, I can lie to myself, but eventually I won't be able to if I keep it up.

I meet her eyes now, and gently ease my fingers off her leg. "Ultimately, it's your decision, but I disagree with it, and I resent that asshole for asking when you have no better options. He's taking advantage, and I want to shoot him in the face for it."

Her eyes flash wide, and she scurries back into the chair. "Well, wait to kill him until after we're married so I can claim the life insurance."

I know she's joking, but the thought of her standing at the altar with him, saying yes, makes me want to do worse than shoot him in the face. We still have time until she has to give him the answer, and I need to use that time to convince her it's a dumb fucking idea. And not just for myself.

I stand and go back to my chair, needing the distance. Even if she makes the choice, I won't let it happen, even if I have to lock her in the bedroom and tie her to the bed. Even Kai couldn't fault me for it if it keeps her from making a choice she might regret for the rest of her life.

"What do you want to do?" I ask, even if it tastes bitter on my tongue.

She shrugs, calm as if it's all a game to her. "I want to meet him again, a little less formally, so we can discuss the advantages and disadvantages together."

Carefully, I exhale, keeping my face neutral, my body calm. It will only give her further reason to say yes if it pisses me off. I've learned that much about her already. "I'll set up another meeting, but we keep it on our turf. I'm not going to him, even if he thinks he's the one helping us."

To this, at least, she nods. "Fine. Can we actually eat dinner this time? If you guys need to have the whole stare down first, fine, but when I go to a nice restaurant, I actually like to enjoy the cooking."

My vision goes red for a flash of a second. This fucking woman. "That is what concerns you? The goddamned food? Not the fact that you might tie your life to a man who is just as guilty as the rest of those damn councilmembers?"

Her mouth thins, and she sits up straight, dropping her feet to the floor with a thud. "Well, I'm glad I understand how you feel about me too. It's obvious you hate all of us equally."

Still riding the anger, I march around the table and get in her face. "Yes, I hate you all, and as far as I'm concerned, they could wipe your entire species from the face of the planet and we'd all be better for it."

Her jaw tightens, her eyes going dark and hooded. "I'll take my food in my room. Set up the meeting. I'd hate to inconvenience you any further than necessary."

I can't breathe until she is out of my sight. Her door slams so loud it rattles the pictures on the wall.

I lie to myself. It's better this way anyway.

12

SELENA

I can still feel the ghost of his fingers on my leg. My skin still tingles with the sensation still. Definitely not a good sign. Maybe I should have put more effort into finding a partner to relieve this ache, someone moldable, biddable, but pretty. Is it still a trophy wife if he's a guy?

My first thought goes to Michail, even though there is nothing biddable about him. He thrives on pushing me until I'm nothing but reaction. Nothing but feeling. No thinking. No logic. And something tells me that's the way he likes people. Leaving them to their base actions, so he can maneuver them however he needs for his own ends.

The problem with being on the receiving end of such manipulation, often you don't even realize you're there, and that he's pushed you too far.

I figured it out as I laid in bed last night thinking about his mouth on mine. He used my own reactions to get me to do what he wanted, leave the bar, and it worked. If those damn full lips hadn't been weaponized against me, I would have found it genius. Tried to talk him into working for me. Now, I'm stuck with the memories and fear of his abilities.

I throw myself back on my bed and pray he stays out of my room long enough to get my brain and my body back on the same page.

"It was one fucking kiss," I murmur to myself. "One kiss isn't worth all this thought."

People kiss other people all the time. Why is this so different? Because it's been years since I've allowed someone to touch me intimately? Because I fear reducing myself to that base level and letting someone else see it, witness me like that?

Right now, I need to think about this meeting with my possible future fiancé. Even the thought in my head sounds wrong. Not that me being married to anyone at all sounds right. Marriage was never in my plans.

Damn them for taking this choice from me. Even without a real choice, is this a better option? I'll be tied to this man for life, or until I decide I'm over him and attempt to kill him. I've always known I wouldn't have the kind of relationship my mother and father had. I just can't trust someone that way. I can never trust someone with all of me.

I roll over on the bed and stare at my suitcase, the one I haven't bothered unpacking. I thought this would take a few days and I'd head home to solidify my power base. At this rate, I'll be stuck with my surly babysitter for weeks. Something neither of us will survive.

But is getting free of Michail's clutches the only reason I'm thinking of joining Emmanuelle? Doesn't seem like a great long-term strategy.

Especially when Michail's touch wakes me up so thoroughly and I couldn't be any more indifferent to Emmanuelle and whatever he's offering. He's handsome, I'll give him that, but his rugged former frat boy vibe doesn't do it for me.

My door bursts open hard enough to hit the wall behind it.

Michail, of course, walks in like he has since we first moved into this hotel suite. "Your meeting is set. You might want to get ready."

I can't help it. I sit up on the bed and glare. "You don't have any whore outfits for me tonight? Nothing that says good luck for your impending marriage?"

"Maybe if you were actually marrying that asshole, but we both know it'll never happen. No matter what you might tell him, or yourself." He saunters closer, his hands casually stuffed into his tailored slacks. "You want to know how I know?"

I shake my head. "No, because I don't care about your opinions. Not when it comes to things you have no right registering an opinion on."

He continues his slow advance forward, and I resist scuttling backward on the bed to keep the distance between us. "If a gunman walked through that door right now, I'd step in front of you. It's my actual fucking job to take a bullet for you, even though I don't even like you."

I narrow my eyes, hoping he can tell I feel the same. I open my mouth to speak, but he grabs my chin in a lightning fast move I can't evade. "No, you're not speaking now, you little brat. If a man walks in here with a gun, I'll protect you, because it's my job, and the job one of my best friend's asked of me. So that, and that alone, entitles me to some opinion about what you'll be doing with your person, at least while you're under my care."

The nerve of this bastard. I try to free my chin, but he only tightens his grip, sliding his thumb up to press on my bottom lip. "No," he whispers. "You're still not talking. Not right now, not while I'm within ten feet of you, or I might toss you out the fucking window."

I clear my throat, his thumb moving across my lips. Despite his order, I speak anyway. "The windows don't open."

"Oh, I can be very creative. You have no idea."

I'm not sure why that statement causes things to tighten my belly, and lower. A wash of heat flits along my bare skin, leaving goosebumps on my legs.

"Why are you so invested in driving me crazy?" he asks, no menace or malice in his voice, not a bit of what has driven him since I first got out of bed.

"You say that like I actually care and consider what you think or want." I match his flat tone.

"Hm." He presses my lips into my teeth until I have to open my mouth for him or risk pain. "That sounds about right. Same as every other councilmember. You don't give a shit about anyone but yourself."

He flirts with sliding his finger between my lips, but abruptly releases me and steps away. "Get ready. We are leaving in a half hour. I won't be waiting for you. If you're not by the door, I'll go down myself and tell this bastard to fuck himself right off a cliff." He walks out of my room without a word or even a look back at where I'm still sitting, flushed and angry.

How dare he? Every step of this journey has been him yelling at me, bodily forcing me around, or complaining about my presence in general. At this rate, I'm not convinced I would have been better off staying in Chicago to deal with everything myself.

"Twenty-nine minutes," he shouts from somewhere beyond my door.

I sigh, forcing all my frustration into a long puff of useless air. It does absolutely nothing to ease my frustration.

With nothing else to do, I get dressed and ensure I'm standing by the door under Michail's deadline.

He gives me a cursory look, and I'm glad I listened to my gut and wore a dress he'd have vetoed off the bat. It's black, and so short I have to be careful how I sit. Best of all, it hugs every inch of my body. It was tailor-made to knock people on their asses, but he barely spares me a glance before throwing open the hotel room door and holding it for me to precede him.

It doesn't matter. I'm not here to impress him, or hell, even this man I'm about to meet with. I dress for myself, and occasionally to weaponize what stiletto heels do to my ass.

Even on the ride down in the elevator, he's quiet, and I can't tell if he's waiting for me to say something or just continuing in his usual dick mode. Either way, I'm not the one who will break the porcelain silence precariously balancing between our pride.

We ride down in silence, and he tugs me out of the elevator, tight fingers wrapped around my bicep. I only allow him to pull me along because he knows where we are going. The second he marches in the crowded restaurant and stops at a table, I jerk my arm from his hold.

With a glare, he unbuttons his suit and pulls the chair out for me. And with an equal glare, I take the seat and meet Emmanuelle's eyes over the white linen tablecloth.

The soft drone of the restaurant around us makes me feel safer. As does Michail at my side, even if I want to punch him in his smug face.

"You're alone tonight," I say, pulling the napkin off my plate to drape over my lap. A server fills water glasses, then wine glasses with whatever Emmanuelle chose before we arrived.

I'm focusing on the councilman when Michail's fingers play down the nape of my neck. I shiver under his touch, my concentration splintering.

"I am. I decided I can do this meeting alone, even if you haven't. I see you still brought your friend with you."

I risk a glance at Michail and find him playing the sulking, jealous lover, looking younger than he has any right to look. Despite the death stares he's casting at Emmanuelle, he's slipped into the part the same as he does every time we are out in public together. It would be disconcerting if I didn't do something similar myself when I'm faced with literally anyone. I don't think my family even knows the real me.

"Well, as you know, there have been many threats on my life. He's not just eye candy…he's functional too."

Michail dips his warm fingers into the top of my dress at the center of my spine. A tingle rolls through me under the patterns he traces against my skin.

"Well, of course, you have to be kept safe," Emmanuelle says, then takes a sip of his wine.

I follow suit, needing some distraction from the situation and from Michail tormenting me with little more than a brush of his fingertips. Am I that hard up for connection? For touch? I'd be better off hiring one of the casino prostitutes. At least they won't mouth off while they help me out.

The councilman gives me an expectant look. Shit. I wasn't paying attention. Michail chuckles softly from beside me. "Forgive me, Councilman. What were you saying?"

"I asked again if you've decided about my proposal."

I clear my throat, ready to answer, when Michail's other hand trails over my knee. Quickly, I shove it away, trying to be as surreptitious as possible, but something tells me Emmanuelle misses very little.

Michail, of course, doesn't take the hint, curling his hand over my bare thigh and sliding it up under my dress. There's no way to pry his fingers loose without alerting Emmanuelle to my problem, so I take another drink of the rich earthy red wine and give him a winning smile. One I've practiced hundreds of times. It says I'll do what you want, but you're not going to like it.

The way Michail's fingers tighten and slide higher, I feel he catches the subtext under the curve of my lips.

"I've actually considered your proposal thoroughly. While it benefits both of us, provided I get out of this little coup alive, and retake my seat, I feel the benefits weigh highly on your side of things. Once we marry, I won't be Selena Aquila anymore. I'll be the councilman's wife, and sweetie, trust me, I am not titled with another person's name."

His eyes narrow, his sharp cheekbones making his face appear more menacing in his anger. "So you are declining, something you could have done over the phone and saved me a trip."

He stands and buttons his suit jacket. When he turns to give us a nod, I pin him with a glare. "Sit down, shut up, and listen. I'm accepting your proposal, but we will have some provisions."

13
MICHAIL

The councilman looks shocked at her tone, and I have to admit, I like the look on him. It also does something to me to hear her bitchy side come out toward others. She can mouth off to anyone she likes, except me.

If she weren't talking about marrying this asshole, this entire situation might even be a bit fun.

I trail my fingers up her spine and dig into the hair curling at the nape of her neck. The councilman's eyes flick to me, then back to Selena as if he wants to say something about me touching her. Interesting.

Instead, he leans back into his chair and throws his arm over the empty one beside him. The picture of rich boredom. "And what might these terms be? I'll need to be aware before I agree, of course."

Beside me, Selena doesn't so much as flinch at the ice in his tone. "Naturally. They are simple. This won't be a real engagement. As much as I love the idea of solidifying and taking power of two cities, we both know I'll never be able to hold power here, not as your wife, and you being a member of the council already."

His eyebrow lifts slightly, acknowledging her point.

"Furthermore," she continues, "you will offer me all the protection I require, whether I am here, or in my city. As well as protection should I need to travel between, or elsewhere."

Now he sits forward and clasps his hands on the table. A silver ring glints on his pinky, some kind of house crest. Studying him closer, now I spot the calluses on his fingers, the faint scars on his face. His rich boy routine is an act. Even more interesting.

I'm wishing I didn't have to kill this man after all.

I turn my focus back to Selena as she continues to outline her terms. "We'll play the parts, pretend, and when I retake my seat and you ascend to yours, we'll maintain an alliance, but drop the engagement. You can break it off, or say you broke it off, anyway you wish."

Emmanuelle's eyes shift to me and narrow. "And if I don't want our relationship to be in name only? What if I want access to your body?"

I tighten my hand on the back of Selena's neck and glare at the councilman, who's staring right back, the same sharp focus in his eyes.

Selena clears her throat. "That is not on the table. We aren't lovers, and I doubt we'd suit anyway. You're far too high-handed for me."

I drag my eyes to the side of her face and smirk. Does she realize how controlling I'll be if I get my hands on her?

I consider a second longer and ease my fingers from her skin. No. I can't afford to be thinking that way. Not while I'm supposed to be doing a job. Not when Kai will skin me alive if he finds out I've even touched her.

She stiffens and shivers but keeps her attention solely on Emmanuelle. "I understand you might think you want me in your bed, but I assure you, you don't. I won't be able to give you the submission you want, and you won't be able to make me feel safe enough to even attempt it. Sex is a vulnerability for a woman in power. It's a lesson I've learned over and over again. Look at your own head councilwoman if you need an example."

Emmanuelle reaches out and clasps Selena's hand. I'm about five seconds from ripping them apart, only holding myself in check so I don't draw attention to us in the middle of the restaurant. He glides his thumb over her knuckles gently. "Who said I need a submissive woman in my bed? The one you saw me with before is no more submissive than your own little friend here."

I don't call him out on his dig. Instead, I tread my fingers up the back of her neck and into her hair again. The heat of her seeps through my suit coat, and her eyes go heavy-lidded.

"Is that it?" Emmanuelle whispers, clutching her hand in both of his now. "You have to be forced into submission to enjoy it. I can do that for you if you need it. Give me a chance to show you. We could be good together, in and out of bed."

She narrows her eyes and shakes me off, so I let my hand fall to the back of her chair, keeping my eyes on the councilman. "I don't need anything, and no one forces me into anything. These are my terms. Are we still in agreement?"

Emmanuelle flicks his eyes to me, and I hold his gaze, challenging him. How badly does he want this? Enough to agree to a complete sham?

Instead, he rises, pulls the ring box from his pocket, and sets it on the table between them. "I have much to consider and will be in touch. For now, though, I expect you to wear this."

Her jaw tightens, and her eyes spark, something I can see even though I'm monitoring her in profile. "You can expect it all you like. We'll see how I feel once things are settled."

With those words, he buttons his coat, slides me a cold look, and walks out of the restaurant. I follow his back until I can't see him in the crowd beyond the opening to the casino floor.

She spins to glare at me, grabs the box, and jams the ring onto her finger. "What the fuck was that? Are you trying to ruin this? He probably wouldn't have even added sex to the deal if you weren't sitting there like a jealous lover about to be cast out of my bed."

The waiter brings a breadbasket, and I snag a roll to chew on, anything to calm me down and keep me from throwing her across the table and fucking her in front of a room full of strangers. After I swallow, I shove my hair away from my face and narrow her a look. "One, watch your fucking mouth. You don't speak to me like that unless you really want me to shove my cock in there and teach you a lesson."

She gasps, her hand coming up to clutch at her chest. "Wh-what?"

"Second, I wasn't ruining anything. The bastard wants you even more now that he knows there's another man interested. Call it fucked up male bullshit, but he does. He'll agree to your terms because he thinks he's good enough, or handsome enough, to seduce you despite what you've told him. He's all ego in a pretty suit."

"And you are, what? Anger and venom wrapped up tight in Armani?"

I wipe my fingers on my napkin and stand. She watches me closely as I toss money on the table, grab her by the arm, and haul her out the backdoor of the restaurant, down a short flight of stairs, and into the tunnels which lead off into the basement.

She stumbles quietly behind me until I drag her into an office, my office, and close the door behind us. It's dark, and she's breathing hard. Hard enough that I can hear every inhale, every exhale and how erratically her heart is beating beneath that sinful little dress of hers.

I pick her up and drop her on the desk. She clutches at my arms, thrown off balance because she didn't see me coming at her. It's the only reason I can rip the ring off her finger and toss it away into the darkened room.

That's his ring. His mark. And something inside me won't allow it to be on her skin. Not when I haven't even marked her for myself yet.

"What the fuck?" she grumbles but staying exactly where I've sat her. "Why are you so fucking crazy?"

"Crazy?" I whisper. "Why am I crazy, you ask? It seems like a dumb ass question since you are so intent on selling yourself to someone who hasn't proven he can keep you safe. You'll buy his protection, but you don't even know if it's worth the cost."

She shrugs and folds her arms under her breasts. "No, but it's a hell of a lot better than being cooped up in a stupid hotel room with nothing to do and no way to take back my city."

I tug her arms away. She resists, but I'm stronger. I arrange her hands on the edge of the desk and curl her fingers down so she grips it. "Keep your hands there, or I'll make you regret it."

Part of me is hoping she disobeys, but she actually listens, her big eyes staring up at me in the dark. I pry her thighs apart and curl my hands around to her hips to pull her to the edge of the desk and take my place between them.

"Is this what you truly want?" I ask, trailing my fingers up her inner thigh until I graze the edge of her lace panties. "You want to sell your soul to keep your body safe? It might sound like a good deal now, but I promise you, without your soul, life is a hell of a lot harder."

I can feel her eyes on my face, trying to read me, figure out what's happening. But I keep my gaze on my fingers, tracing the soft lace. "Without your soul, you slowly lose more and more, like it's the container that holds you all together. First, your morals, then your compassion, and finally, your heart."

She shakes her head mournfully. "I'm already missing all of those things anyway, so maybe he's getting the raw end to this deal."

I shake my head and bring my other hand to trail the other edge of the lace. "No, you only like to think you don't have a heart. You sought protection when people took what's yours. You even tried to throw the old hag councilwoman off Kai's scent, despite playing the spoiled brat to everyone else. If there's one thing I can spot a mile away, it's an act."

She huffs and grabs my hands to pry them away. I curl her fingers over the edge of the desk again, staring into her eyes now. "Last warning, move again, and you'll regret it."

She gulps and nods. I dig my fingers into the lace right over her pussy and rip the fabric wide open, a hole from seam to seam so I can touch her bare skin. My fingers glance over soft curls, but I'm going for the sweetness below. She's soaked, and yet, she looks as composed as if she's waiting for a bus.

"You are dripping all over my hand, and there's nothing on your face," I note, more for me than her.

"What can I say? I've got a good poker face, and who says that's for you? Maybe I find the councilman attractive. He offered to take me to his bed after all."

Now she's just goading me. I cup my hand over her heat, learning the shape of her, then dip my thumb in to flick along her clit.

She hisses out a breath, her body jerking. "What-what do you think you're doing?"

I flick the little nub again, enjoying how her tight little cunt wets my hand further with her arousal. I can smell her now, and I want so much more than a little taste.

"You want to sell yourself for your protection? That's up to you, I suppose. There's nothing I can do about it except lock you up. But something tells me you'll come to resent me for that if I do."

She gulps, sending primal satisfaction through me. "Yes." Her hips move forward the tiniest bit as her body seeks the friction it craves.

I give her cunt one proprietary slap, causing her to jump, and take a step away from her. Fuck me, I can smell her, and my cock is an iron bar in my pants. But she can't see any of that, so I keep my voice even. "Fine, you want to sell yourself for protection, then you can start with me, and I take payment up front."

14

SELENA

Why is it that every time Michail manhandles me, I want him more? I lie in bed late into the night, and most of the next day, trying to figure it out. All the while, continuing to hide from him. Every time I move, the damn ring Emmanuelle gave me reminds me of the choice I was forced to make, and likely what I'll soon regret.

I'd taken it off, but when I sat at the table to eat breakfast, Michail refused to feed me until I put it back on. Like both of us needed the token to remember what happened between us after my agreement to marry Emmanuelle.

My stomach rumbles. The clock tells me it's almost time for dinner, and I'm wondering if I can get a drink to go with it. Something to dull all the shit going on in my brain right now. But I doubt His Majesty will allow even that concession. He lives to piss me off.

It might not even be worth it to leave my room. If I wait long enough, I can sneak out later and grab something when he's off, I don't know, breathing down someone else's neck.

I barely have time to reconsider, my stomach growling, when Michail marches into my room, without knocking, as usual.

He tosses another skimpy bit of material on the bed then sits a tray of food beside it. "Eat, get dressed. We are going down to the floor tonight. We have some work to do."

His eyes are cold today, his curls swept away from his face in disarray, like he's been combing his fingers through them. "You have a half hour to meet me at the door."

I glare and stay on my side on the bed. "I heard you. You can go now."

Grinding his jaw, he spins and walks out. I'll pay for my attitude later, I'm sure. His Highness doesn't like to be disrespected. I sit up and feel the silky fabric. It's navy-blue tonight, so at least I have shoes to match since he didn't leave me any.

I move the tray into my lap, scarf down the vegetable stew, and then head into the bathroom to dress. I don't have time to wash my hair, so I put it up with a couple of hair sticks and leave a few strands hanging around my face. It takes me longer to get into the skintight dress than it does to finish my makeup. In the end, I slip on my shoes and walk out to meet him at the door. He's standing there in a black-on-black suit, his hair slicked back, checking his watch.

I turn to face away from him. "Can you zip this, please? I swear if the dresses you give me get any smaller, I'll be better off just walking out of here naked."

His hands are warm against the bare skin of my back, and I suppress a shudder. I also ignore the way my heart picks up a heavy beat until his warmth and scent move away again.

I turn to face him, jaw tense. "Well, let's get this over with. Can I get a drink with whatever fresh hell you've got planned for tonight?"

He opens the door without a word and motions for me to go first. But I barely pass him when he snags my hand, rips the ring off it, and drops it into his front pocket. There's no use questioning him, so I keep going. In the hall, we walk to the elevator and step inside. Every damn time we get into the steel, mirror lined box, my heart rate doubles.

As usual, he shakes out his shoulders, straightens, then wraps his arm around my waist to pull me in close. "Put on your game face so we can get to work."

I want to pry his fingers off me, mostly because I feel even more unsteady when he's touching me, but I don't. Instead, I plaster on a dim-witted smile and lean into him. Just in time for the doors to slide open, revealing the hotel lobby and the start of the casino floor.

He leads me around the machines, his fingers tightening on my waist so I can only hold on to him in return, stumbling along in my heels.

When we reach the club, the music is blaring, a thumping bass which reaches into me, vibrating me from head to toe. It only takes a few minutes to get to the VIP section, the same one we occupied last time, and take our seats.

A server brings a bottle of whiskey, some ice, and two glasses. Michail hands her some bills, and she disappears.

I point at the glasses and wrap my left thigh over his. "Want to pour me a drink, lover?"

He doesn't miss a beat, leaning forward to pour us both a couple fingers of whiskey, then drop two ice cubes in each glass.

I reach out to take it from him, but he brings the glass to my lips, his eyes steady, heated, on mine. "Drink."

Unable to slap him, or his hand away, I latch onto his wrist, lick the edge of the highball glass where a drop of liquid slipped over, then let him pour the alcohol onto my tongue.

When it's gone, he swigs back the other glass and slides them onto the low table again. "Keep your ears open," he whispers into my neck. Then leaves a little bite that zips through my system faster than the alcohol did. In seconds, I'm wet and aching. Fuck him and how easily he gets to me.

I curl my leg to slide my knee up his thigh, almost to his crotch. "What am I listening for?"

His warm fingers splay over my bare leg, leading up almost to the outside edge of the dress, barely covering my ass in this position. "Anything that would be helpful."

I swallow hard, wanting another drink to either curb this ache or fan the embers into a flame. If I'm going to be consumed by him, it might as well be on my terms, not his.

I shift so I can straddle him, and his hands keep my dress from riding up too high. I lean in and bite his earlobe, the scent of lemongrass enveloping me, teasing me. "Well, if we are listening, I caught some words to our left."

He gently runs his hands over my ass and up my back while we both listen. There are two men, but I can't see them well enough to identify them, not that I'd be able to identify many here in another territory, outside of straight councilmembers and their families.

The one man is talking louder, making our jobs easier.

"I heard she captured Kai, the Doubeck second, and tortured him."

The other man snorts and takes a sip, maybe. I can't tell over the music, but the tinkling of ice makes me think so. "I heard she tied him to her bed and raped him."

It's the first man's turn to snort, adding a deep chuckle. "You can't rape a man. We call that no strings attached sex in my world."

I stiffen, putting the pieces together. Michail's hands tighten on my waist, pulling me all the way against him. "Just listen. Don't give yourself away. We'll get more by monitoring, not fighting."

I lean in so my mouth almost touches his. "That man is talking about my brother. Saying someone raped my brother."

Michail's eyes go from heated to chilled in less than a second. "Yeah, and that's the world you're so desperate to get back to. The world where the privileged take what they want from the rest of us, no matter what the damage is."

I jerk backward, forcing him to release me as I climb off his lap. "I'm going to the bar to get a drink. I won't leave your sight, but I need a minute, or else I'll do something that will break our cover."

He pins me with a look until I shuffle off to the bar, tugging my dress down and rearranging my boobs so I'm not about to pop out the top. At the bar, a server comes quickly, but so do three other working girls. They crowd close, their hips touching mine, their perfume almost choking me.

"Are you here with Michail?"

I sigh, barely keeping myself from rolling my eyes and saying something snarky. Instead, I paste on a dim smile and bat my lashes. "Sure, he seems to like me."

The bleached-blonde girl to my right, who desperately needs a toner, scowls at me. The other two wiggle in excitement. "Oh, my gosh, how did you snag him? Everyone tries when he comes here, but no one gets any of them."

Two glasses slide toward me, and I catch them, one in each hand, but my focus is on the surrounding women. "Them? What do you mean, them?"

The brunette leans in and looks around like she's about to impart state secrets. "Adrian's guys. We used to see Ivan all the time." Her voice takes on a wistful note. "I almost caught his interest once, but we rarely see the rest of them. Hell, I'd even take the chick, Andrea."

I recall the statuesque woman I'd met a few days ago. Most people would. She's stunning. "I better get back over there before he comes to hunt me down."

Bleached blonde scowls harder and nudges me, sending my drinks clattering to the bar. I glare but scoop them up again and head back toward Michail. That one has her eyes on him for sure. Did they have a history?

When I sit beside him, he takes one drink and throws it back like it's nothing. I hold mine in my lap. "The blonde at the bar has the hots for you, and the brunette has her eyes on your friends, including Andrea."

He narrows his eyes and scans them, where they aren't being subtle about watching us. "Oh, really? Is that all they said?"

I take a sip of the drink and shrug. "Yeah, it's all I let them say before blondie over there tried to take me out with a very ample hip check."

His eyes drift down, and I elbow him hard. "Really? You're checking them out while I'm sitting right here?"

"Go back over, see if they say anything else?"

I chuckle but stop when I catch sight of his completely serious expression. "You really want me to go over there and pretend to be a prostitute?"

He hefts me up to stand and slaps my ass hard. "You've been pretending since we left the elevator. Or maybe since you agreed to marry Emmanuelle?"

I grind my jaw and turn my back, heading to the place at the bar again.

The tall, too thin woman on the other side of the brunette speaks as I approach. "Oooh, trouble in paradise already? Why don't one of us give it a try? See if we can make him happy."

I belly up to the bar, leaning my elbows on it. "You could try, but his penis is so small, it might not be worth the effort."

The brunette snickers, and the bleached blonde scowls at me. "You're lying. I can always tell when a man is packing, and that one is definitely packing."

I shrug and motion for a shot. If I have to stay here with the three stooges, I might as well get something out of it. Also, it wouldn't hurt to keep my mind off the fact that I know there is nothing small about Michail.

"You're not telling us, are you?" Blondie asks. "You're just keeping him for yourself and depriving us of a chance."

I turn to look at him over my shoulder. He narrows his eyes. "You can have him, honey. His brand of crazy isn't worth the effort."

A slight buzz is setting in, which is why I don't see the blonde's claws heading for my face.

She doesn't reach me as Michail smoothly steps between us, catching her hand and roughly shoving her away. "Don't touch what belongs to me."

He scoops me in tight, making me fumble my next shot, losing it on the bar as he drags me through the VIP section to the back.

15

MICHAIL

I don't know what's gotten into me, but the moment that bastard laid claim to her, I haven't been able to flip the switch in my head, the switch that makes it so simple to don the mask and pretend I couldn't care less.

I drag her beside me until I find an empty room. The door bounces against the frame from the force of my push.

Selena stumbles into the dark while I take a moment to close and lock the door properly.

I flip the light switch and blink against the glaring overhead light. Each movement slow, calculated, drawing out time so I can calm the fuck down. She's hugging herself and glaring at the same time, like she can repel me with just the look she's giving me.

"What are you—?"

I cut her off. "Shut up."

Her glare shifts from icy to nuclear. "You don't—"

This time I cut her off with my mouth, my lips mashed against hers in the most artless kiss imaginable. Which I rectify when I spear my fingers into her hair and hold her face to mine. Her hands come up and cup my elbows, and she digs her nails into my suit jacket as if it can keep her grounded.

Fuck. She tastes like sin and whiskey and everything I know I can't have. I delve deeper into her mouth, forcing her lips apart to get a better taste. Her moan slices my control to shreds, and I walk her back to the empty desk behind her. When she stops at the piece of furniture, I pick her up, our lips still locked together, and sit her on the edge.

She pulls away from me with a gasp, but fuck that, I haven't had enough of her yet. If I'm going down in flames, I'm going to light my own damn match. Things end when I say they do.

I capture her head more firmly this time, cradling her cheek in one hand, cupping the back of her neck with the other. This time I kiss her properly, teasing her tongue with mine, starting out slow until she's whimpering and straining to touch me.

When her hands curl around my lapels, I release her head and cover them. I pry her grip loose and pull both my mouth and my body away. My dick is so hard, I think I've lost circulation from the fit of my slacks, and right now, I'm two seconds from ripping that barely there dress off her body and fucking her until the desk breaks.

She blinks heavily and gulps. "What the hell was that?"

I shake my head and try to get a hold of myself. When we came in here, I meant to teach her a lesson. Demonstrate what I meant by paying up front for my protection. Then her damn mouth distracted me.

I adjust my suit jacket and square my shoulders. It takes a second to force the words past the boulder in my throat. "We should get back out there. We still have work to do here."

Her jaw tenses, and she hops off the desk to glare at me. "Fine, I'm not the one who dragged you in here."

She skirts me and heads toward the door. I follow, imagining how satisfying her ass will look marked up with my red handprints.

We get back to our booth, and she curls in beside me, leaving a few inches of distance, but I've already switched my mask, the playboy, the rich idiot, out for a night with a little easy company.

She glances at my face, and then does a double take, like she hasn't seen me slip into a role several times before right now. "How do you do that? Why do you do that?"

I lean in and nibble her earlobe. "Do what?"

Her breath stutters. "How do you look like a completely different person from one moment to the next? I swear if I weren't here with you, I might not have seen it."

Her fingers tremble, and she tucks them together into her lap, but I'm not letting her off that easily. "Go grab us another round, and maybe I'll tell you."

She spots the other working girls at the far end of the bar. "You want me to go back over there? Why don't we just get the server?"

I sprawl my arms over the back of the booth and splay my legs wide. Manspreading, Andrea calls it. "Because I told you to, doll. Go grab us a couple of drinks, and I'll explain what you asked."

For a second, her only response is a glare, then she slides from the half-circle booth, and goes to the bar.

I keep my eyes on the other girls in case they bother her again. The blonde spots her in an instant and heads right for her. Interesting, she'd go after Selena when she could just come to me, knowing I'm alone.

The blonde hip-checks Selena, and I've had about enough of this woman. I stand and reach the bar in a second. "What's taking so long?" I ask, cutting between Selena and the blonde, who doesn't move an inch, leaving her body plastered against the back of mine.

She glares at the blonde, then the bartender sits our drinks in front of her. "It's fine. They are right here. Why don't we go sit down?"

I level her a look, hoping she reads it, and after a few tense seconds, she does. Her tone turns syrupy and dim. "Come on, baby.

We're wasting time over here when we can do so many things that are much more fun."

I lick my lips and move to follow her, but a hand on my shoulder stops me. The blonde, leaning over the bar. "When is your friend coming back?"

I shrug off her grip, keeping my eyes cold. "I don't know what you mean. I don't have any friends."

She narrows her eyes, leaning in. "The dark one, with all the tattoos. Looks like he's going to eat you or end you, and you're not sure which you prefer."

I file away that colorful description and scan her features. She looks stone sober, and maybe a little sad. "I think you mean, Ivan. He'll be back when my business here concludes."

She slides her gaze toward Selena and back at me. "Well, I hope it ends quickly. Tell him Penny has missed him."

On that note, I walk the few steps back to our booth and curl up against Selena again. She's staring the blonde down, and I appreciate her level of commitment. For a second, I thought I spotted jealousy in her gaze.

Another second passes until she can't help herself. "What did she want?"

I sip my drink, scanning the crowd for any familiar faces. "Nothing much, just asking after Ivan."

She leans in and runs her hand down my chest. "The crazy one?"

"Not sure what that means…" To me, he's just Ivan. My friend and fellow protector.

She giggles, and it's high and flirty, nothing like the deep throatiness of her real laugh. "You know what they say about you guys…right?"

I meet her eyes, waiting, since she obviously wants to tell me.

"Adrian, the monster. Kai, the playboy." She makes a disgusted face at Kai's descriptor. "You are the mystery, and Ivan is usually called the animal or the crazy one, and…"

"And what?" I'm curious what her society set calls the twins.

"They call Andrea and Alexei fire and ice. Him being the one who runs hot and angry and well, slutty. Her vengeance is colder and more calculated. I can appreciate that in a woman. I was happy to have finally met her the other night."

She would appreciate Andrea's cold practicality. It hurts me to think about how the twins have turned into this version of themselves. They are the youngest of the Five and should be the least burdened. Everything that's happened in the past year has changed us all.

I keep my eyes on the crowd, even though I want to meet her eyes, see what she really thinks. "The mystery. Hm...maybe only to those lucky enough not to have met me. Then again, most of the people who have met me are no longer speaking."

She stiffens in my arms, and I take the opportunity to lift her and pull her across my lap. "So why are you protecting me, then? Why didn't Kai send someone else to watch me?"

I shrug and trail my fingers up her thigh until I meet the hem of her dress. "I don't know, but for now, you're all mine, and I believe I'm owed for protecting you a little bit ago."

Her forehead wrinkles as she meets my eyes. "You mean from the prostitute I could have knocked out with one punch? You didn't save me; you saved her. And she looks more than happy to pay you in whatever way you see fit."

I shift her on my lap so she's straddling me. "Not happening, but in my mind, you owe me for saving you at the bar, at your house, and all the time in between I've kept you safe."

Her mouth drops open, and I immediately stick two fingers inside and hold her chin with my thumb. When her eyes blaze and her teeth push against my skin, I shake my head softly. "Nope, you bite me, and I bite you back. Keep that in mind.

Gently, I shove the table with my free hand to give her some space and slide her to the floor.

She swallows hard, and her tongue slides along the underside of my fingers. I'm still hard from kissing her earlier, so it's nothing to ensure the table is covering us both as I unbuckle my pants.

I gently remove my fingers from between her lips and use both hands to get my aching dick out. "Now, be a good girl and suck it."

Her eyes blaze as she stares up at me from the darkness around my legs. "You have got to be kidding me?" But even in her anger, I can see the pink in her cheeks, the way she licks her lips like she can't help but give herself a taste.

"Go ahead. I'm not the kind of man you want to owe a debt to."

She leans in, and my cock twitches as her warm breath fans over it. "Why are you making me do this?"

I pull the ring from my jacket pocket and show it to her. "Because you made it perfectly clear you are fine with selling yourself for protection, so why should he get the benefits and none of dealing with your bratty mouth? At least now, when I deal with your bratty mouth, I'll get some benefits too."

She glares again. "I fucking hate you."

I sprawl again, looking completely at ease to anyone who might wander by our table. "You can hate me and suck my dick. They aren't mutually exclusive. We don't have all night, Princess."

She scowls again and roughly grabs me but pauses like she expects me to admonish her. I don't. There's nothing she can do to me that hasn't been done to me countless times before, in both pleasure and pain.

It takes her another minute of working herself up to lean over and take the head of me between her lips. I keep my face neutral, composed. This is nothing more than a business arrangement, after all.

She slides down my length as far as she can, and I resist the urge to thrust up to get deeper into the warm dream that is her mouth. When she adds her hand, I can't keep my knees from shaking.

Just as I'm about to reach down and haul her off me, someone slides into the booth on my right.

I glance up, a *fuck off* already on my lips when Ivan gives me a wide smile. "Well, where's the little princess you're supposed to be babysitting?"

16

SELENA

I don't know if staying where I am or climbing out from under the table is the best option. I'm still holding him, his dick between my lips and my hand on his shaft.

It would be a lie to say I hate this. What I hate is that I can't hear a word they are saying over the music. After the first few words, they pitched their voices low, too low to hear from my vantage point.

I lean forward and suck him deep. Fine. If he wants to keep me trapped down here, I'll make him pay for it. Let's see him have a business meeting while I suck his soul out through his cock.

My knees ache, so I shift to take some of the weight off and get a pinch on my arm for my effort.

The bastard. I scrape my teeth gently from as far as I can get up his shaft until I bite gently on the head and pop him out of my mouth. If he knows what's good for him, he won't pinch me again. It would be too easy to shove his legs aside and climb out from under the table. Something tells me he wouldn't enjoy explaining this situation to my brother. To be fair, neither would I.

The light is low, but I take a moment to stare at him. He's thick in my grasp, long and hard, with a slight bend at the tip. Even his damn cock is gorgeous. Figures.

I readjust my grasp and trace the head of him over my lips. He tastes salty, and I lick the slit and then suck him down as far as I can get in my throat.

I can't hear his words above the table, but his voice falters for a second, his friend's tone turns questioning.

A little zip of pride bursts in my chest like a sparkler. A tiny spark flares brighter, and I push my boundaries, taking him down my throat so far, I almost gag.

His knees quake around my biceps, his thighs tense. I brace my hand on one thick muscular thigh and bring my hand up from the base of him to meet my lips with each deep slow suck.

I've always been so indifferent about blow jobs, but this one is different. It makes me feel powerful in a way I've never felt before. I've reduced this stunning man to quaking, and I want more.

So much more.

I lean into him, tilting my head to take him deeper, relaxing my jaw. His legs shake under my hold, and his hand comes down to tense on my shoulder.

I freeze for a heartbeat, waiting. If he pinches me again, he'll regret it.

Instead, he curls his hand behind my head and into the hair at the nape of my neck. To his credit, he doesn't push or try to move me. It's like he just wants me to know he's with me.

For that, I try to take him deeper and faster. Something's changed. If this is meant to be a punishment, I'll take it any day. The taste of him is intoxicating. The sense of power I feel is a drug all its own.

There's some shifting by the other man. I can't see him, but his knee nudges the base of the table, which is hiding me. Then silence.

I stop and lift my lips from Michail. Just in time for him to tuck himself away and then drag me up into the booth beside him.

"You can manhandle me a little less. That would be nice," I manage as I wipe my mouth on my forearm.

His eyes are dark with fire, his lips turned down as his strong jaw flexes. "Let's go."

I'm tempted to lean back in the booth, move slowly, and deny him. But the wicked hot pulse in my body, in my nipples, in my clit spurs me out of the seat beside him. He takes my hand, weaving our fingers together, and leading me out of the club to the elevator.

The shift in noise is jarring, but I keep my focus on him. What's going to happen now? Will he lick me? Fuck me? Do I want that? I don't even have to pretend in my mind. I want his hands on me more than I want to prop up my pride.

We stand in tense silence, his hand still tucked with mine. Nothing but the soft whine of the elevator between us.

He drags me out of the elevator to our door, opens it with a jerk and shoves it hard, as if he wants to slam it. The piston at the top whooshes, but slowly closes the door.

Now that we are alone, doubt creeps through my chest as I tug my hand from his grip. "What was that all about? Were you putting on a show for your friend, or..."

His back is to me, only the city lights outside cut the darkness of our shared living space. It glances off his curls and the hard edge of his shoulders.

I study his back, waiting for him to answer, or murder me, or hell, throw me back to my knees and shove his dick in my face again. I know which one my traitorous pussy is voting for.

A heartbeat passes, then he turns, grabs my forearm, and once again drags me behind him toward his bedroom door this time. We enter, and I stare around the space I've barely had a glimpse of since we checked in. The room is the mirror image of mine, except his is tidy in a way mine won't be unless I actually make an effort to clean up.

I indulge my curiosity and keep looking around. There are stacks of books on most flat surfaces, all neat, ordered by size. Even his bed is perfectly made, and I know for a fact the maids only drop off towels. They don't actually clean anything.

He drops my arm and spins to face me, then flips on the lamp beside his bed.

With rough jerks, he strips his suit jacket off and lays it over the armchair in the corner. Then he works the tie at his throat to strip it off, adding it to the jacket.

I keep my eyes on him, the slow revealing of his body. Each motion precise, heating my already boiling blood even more.

"What do you want?" I whisper, having no idea what he'll say or what he'll do next.

His voice is rough and deeper than usual when he answers. "What do you want, Selena? What the hell was that back there?" There's a fine sharp edge to his tone, anger honed to a keen point.

I let my mouth flop open, sputtering on his reaction, and the wash of my desire fading under the force of that anger. "Are you kidding me? You're the one who shoved me under the table to request your so-called payment."

The heartbeat pulsing through me completes its shift from arousal to anger. "You don't get to be outraged when I do exactly what you forced me to do."

He sputters, charging forward to get into my face. "I didn't force you to do anything you obviously wanted to do."

I raise my hand to slap him, but he catches my wrist mid-motion and drags me into his body. The heat of him folds around me, weakening my resolve.

"You will not hit me." He growls low in my face, his lips an inch from mine. "You have no right to raise your hand to me."

His eyes dip down, then back up to meet mine. "Now, where were we?"

I jerk my wrist from his hold, and he releases me to stumble back. "We aren't anywhere. I'm heading to bed."

He again slides his gaze down, this time to my breasts, my hips, my thighs. "So you're saying if I touched you right now, you wouldn't be absolutely dripping for me?"

I gulp. I'm prey, caught in a hunter's gaze. "It's none of your business if I am or not."

He shrugs lightly. "Maybe I can help?"

It's my turn to scoff, even as my heart is testing the restraint of my body. "I thought we established you're a virgin. I'm pretty sure I can take care of myself better than you can."

His full lips curl at the edges. *Challenge accepted* that smile says. "How about we make a bet? If I make you come, you finish what you started downstairs."

I step into him, my chest brushing against him. "And when you don't?"

The little lift in his lips gets higher. "Then I'll owe you one favor. And I always keep my word."

I shouldn't trust it, but that heartbeat has returned to my body as the scent of him stokes the heat in my belly.

"What do you want me to do?" I ask, a little ashamed of the need in my voice.

"Ask me to make you come."

The words rip through me. This fucking bastard.

"Are you fucking joking?"

"No."

Fuck him. I don't need him to get off.

I sink down to the floor, keeping my eyes on him, enjoying the way his jaw tenses as he watches me.

On my knees, I wiggle the short dress up to my waist and sink back onto my ass. I can't look at him as I slide my hand into my panties, spearing my fingers along my soaked seam. A jolt of pleasure rocks me, my skin more sensitive than it has ever been.

I lean back on my elbows to lie flat on the floor, then place my feet flat and spread my thighs. His fucking loss right now.

I close my eyes and circle my clit softly. A tiny part of my brain knows it would feel better with his fingers on me, but I won't give him the satisfaction.

I bite my bottom lip and ride the sensation, wringing it from my body with each practiced touch.

Something hot grazes my thigh, and I pop my eyes open. He's flat on his belly between my thighs, a knife in his grip.

A bolt of need strikes hard, sizzling me from the inside out. He cuts through my panties, ripping them away. Then he slams the knife into the floor, so it sticks straight up. I can't look away while he lowers his face, spreads me open with one hand and dives face-first into my pussy.

His tongue is unforgiving. He uses the flat of it to lick me from hole to clit and back again. I shake and drop my head onto the floor, unable to hold myself up under the onslaught.

Two fingers spear me, and he keeps lapping at my wet flesh, his fingers moving in time with his tongue. This is so much better than my own fingers and my carefully curated toy collection.

I clench my fists, refusing to touch him, and let him take me where I want to go. Each pass of his hot tongue takes me closer and closer. I can feel the orgasm coming, and it threatens to consume me. I don't even care. I've forgotten everything else except his mouth on my body.

I come with a flash, another lightning strike of pleasure. It blasts through me, sloughing away the indifference, the shame, the pride, all of it, leaving the quivering vulnerable parts of me exposed.

A hot tear slides down my cheek, and I grab his hair, easing him away.

He lets up, shifting to his knees. I can't look at him as I drag my dress down my hips. I can't look at him as I wobble to my feet. I can't look at him as I stop at the door and say, "I'll remit my payment tomorrow."

I close the door behind me and stop, needing the distance.

When I hear the sound of retching from the other side, my newly-bared heart aches for a moment.

What the hell did we do?

17

MICHAIL

I let things go too far. My intention was to scare her. Show her what it means to pay for protection, the way so many people have had to do. It wasn't a pretty decision made under symphony music and champagne. There weren't diamonds and hors d'oeuvres. We had to fight, scrape, and serve in the lowliest ways for the tiniest bit of protection offered to us. If protection could even describe what we paid for.

I rub absently at the scars on the back of my hand, my stomach in knots as I wait for her to come out for breakfast. It has been an hour, and I haven't even heard her moving around in there.

Yesterday, I might have barged in to check on her, but today, I can't face her. Not when I can still taste her, smell her, feel her body quivering for my touch.

I can still taste the vomit in the back of my throat too, even after I brushed my teeth multiple times. It's been years since I've had that reaction to touching another person. I thought I was over it, but this time it wasn't about touching her. It's about what I forced her into, what I forced her to do in the name of teaching her a lesson.

Guilt gnaws through my gut, threatening to send me back to my knees on the bathroom tile. Shame follows, tilling things up inside me better left buried.

We spend three more days circling each other. Anytime we end up in the same room, we avert our gazes and retreat to opposite corners. We don't speak about what happened, or at all, really.

For some reason, it stings, like someone took a cheese grater to my lungs every time I see her. Each look she throws my way has barbs, and worse, I'd endure so many more to taste her one more time. To feel her body quaking under my grasp.

I've licked a lot of cunts in my day. When I got old enough for women to request me specifically, I got good at it, perfecting my skills so they didn't ask for more, take more than I could survive giving up. For the first time, I actually enjoyed it. Each shiver and tremor I inspired spurred my arousal on.

But after my trip to the toilet, I didn't allow myself the release my body craved.

Even three days later, I feel the need to take myself in hand and relieve the ache deep in my gut.

I can't live like this. If anything, I'm more inspired to find out who is trying to take over her world so I can send her home. So far, my list is short, and I have little access to a few of the names there. At some point, we'll have to return to Chicago and face things head on. I'm not ready to deal with that landscape yet, not until I can identify every piece on the board.

I sit alone at the breakfast table for the fourth day in a row. This time, talking myself into checking on her, when my phone rings.

I snatch it up and press it to my ear. "Hello?" Only Adrian and the Five have this number, so I'm never worried about checking the caller ID.

"You still at the casino?" Kai answers.

I keep my eyes on her door. "Where else would I be?"

Kai snorts softly. "Well, come back to the penthouse. We'll review the details and regroup."

My brain slides over his words, snagging on each one like the rough edge of stone. "What?"

"Did I stutter? Pack your shit, grab my sister, get in the car, and drive to the penthouse. What about that didn't you understand?"

He's being short, and that worries me even more. "Why now? We've been here for a while. What's changed?"

He huffs low in his throat. "It's something we can discuss when you get here. For now, just do as you're ordered."

Technically, Adrian is my boss, but he sends dictates through Kai often enough that I don't question it again.

"We'll be there soon. You know how light your sister travels. She'll need a few minutes to pack." Kai makes a noise like he wants to argue, but I cut in before he can. "You want to tell her to leave her belongings, because even I'm not brave enough to do it?"

"Fine, we'll see you when you get here."

He hangs up without a goodbye, and I slide my phone back on the tabletop. Shit.

We are currently sitting in a tangled mess of webs. There is a lot of unwinding Selena and I both need to do before we go back to the penthouse.

I stand, button my jacket, and march to her door. Since she won't answer anyway, I don't bother with knocking.

When I enter, I scan the room, spotting her on the bed, curled on her side in her underwear and a t-shirt. There's a book propped in front of her.

"What?" she says, not even glancing up from the pages.

Any other time, I might find this image the sexiest thing I've seen in a very long time. But there's a pendulum hanging over our heads, and I'd like to keep it on my neck for now.

"We are leaving. Pack your stuff."

She looks up. "What?"

"We've been called to the penthouse. Your brother wants us there immediately."

She presses her lips together, her forehead crumpling. "Why?"

I'm two seconds from running out the door or throwing her back on the bed and climbing between those plush thighs again. I grip the wood of the frame to ground myself. "He didn't deign to give me an explanation. If you want one, you'll have to call him yourself."

She glances at her phone on the bedside table, then back at me. "I think I'll pass on that one. How long do we have? Can we stall for a couple of days?"

I push away from the door to get closer to her. It's easier to read her eyes the closer I get. "Why would we stall?"

She shoots me a dart of a look. "You want to come up with a story on the fly? Explain about us...um...being more intimate with each other than we should be?"

"There's no reason we have to say anything." I slip my hands into my pockets and enjoy seeing all her smooth skin on display.

"You don't think my brother won't spot something is off the second he sees us?"

I shrug, pretending indifference I don't feel at all. "I'm an excellent actor, Selena. Kai only sees what I want him to see. On *my* face, at least."

Her lips flatten and her eyes narrow. "Are you implying I'll rat us out to my brother? There are definitely things I think we'd be better off keeping to ourselves. But..." She shifts to sit up, sliding her legs together and running her hands over her knees. "What is my silence worth to you?"

A hot cut of anger slices through me. "Are you fucking kidding? You want to barter for my silence over something you don't even want him to know in the first place?"

It's her turn to feign indifference, and I can tell she's faking it. She's been pretending since day one. "He won't cut *my* throat for sleeping with you. I can't say the same in reverse. I might not agree with it, but I know how to get what I need out of any situation."

I blink, letting the mask slip over my features more fully. My usual beautiful-boy-without-a-brain act. "And what do you need, Brat? Besides your ass whipped until it's red."

She wiggles like the idea isn't totally unappealing. My hands ache to touch her, but I don't let her see a single bit of it.

Something dark slides into her eyes. Pain maybe? "I want to know why the fuck you puked your guts out after going down on me the other day? I want to know what I did to make you treat me that way. You didn't even wait until I'd gotten far enough that I didn't have to hear it."

I clench my fists, never having to hold on to my mask more than I do right now. "It wasn't about you. It had nothing to do with you at all."

She tilts her head. "And how am I supposed to believe that? Especially when you're wearing that face."

I give her a lazy smile, a default for me, as I think about what she's asking. A dazzling distraction. "You can believe what you want to believe. That's on you, not me. I'm not here to stroke your ego, or make you feel like a princess again. It doesn't matter. It shouldn't have happened anyway."

It's the wrong thing to say. The second the words leave my mouth, I know.

She shoots to her feet, her hands clenched. "Well, we don't want to keep Kai waiting, do we?"

She stalks to the bathroom and slams the door loud enough to rattle the art on the adjacent wall. It's a good thing they bolt those bastards in, or else they'd have hit the floor with how much awareness she shows when she's throwing around all that attitude.

I flex my hand, only allowing this tiny departure, then head to my room to pack up.

It takes me only a few minutes to grab what I need. This room is mine permanently when I stay at the casino, so I don't need to move anything but a few weapons and some clothes.

When I finish, I wait by the door for her to exit her room. She drags her bags out one by one, and I simply watch, letting her stew in anger and pride instead of asking for help.

The driver comes up to take our bags, and I escort her down to the car, my eyes scanning the crowd for anything out of place. But we pass through the lobby without incident.

Every time I go to the penthouse, I feel torn. It's home, but it's also so many walls to keep me inside. Both in structure and obligation.

One day, I'll pay back Adrian for what he did for me. Until then, I follow orders and be the man Adrian needs for anything.

I've learned to be a shadow. His shadow. And everyone knows to fear the dark.

We land in the foyer with a pile of her bags. I have one over my shoulder, and this time I grab hers without her prompting. She cuts me a glare and steps forward, uncertainty written all over her face.

Kai wanders in from the hallway, his suit perfect, a lollipop tucked in the corner of his mouth. "Took you guys long enough, fuck."

I tip my head toward Selena's bags. "As I said."

She glares between us, her ponytail spinning with the movement. "You have a room for me, or am I staying here in the foyer for the duration of my ordered stay?"

Kai's jaw tenses as he studies us, then locks his eyes on his sister. "I see you're in one piece, so Mick must have done his job."

She shrugs her bags off her shoulders to let them fall with the rest. "I'm alive if that's what you're asking. At least for now. Not that we know who is trying to take over my seat. Not that I've been able to make any progress for weeks."

Kai steps up and easily scoops up her bags . "Let's go. I'll take you to the room we set aside. It's yours while you are here."

I follow them both, keeping my eyes off her round ass and on the back of Kai's head.

"I'm glad you two are back. We can plan better now that some of the immediate danger has passed," he says, loud enough that it echoes in the hallway back to me.

We stop outside a door a couple down from his, a peach bedroom for guests, for the very few times someone else stays in the penthouse. I drop the bags outside the door and head toward my room.

Kai calls my name. "Wait. You both need to explain to me how my sister ended up engaged to that council douchebag. Neither of you are leaving until that happens."

18

SELENA

*K*ai storms out of the room before I can offer an explanation. Not that he deserves one. It's not his life, nor him marrying "that council douchebag," as he so eloquently put it. By his look, Michail agrees with his assessment.

They left together with my bags strewn around the door so I couldn't close it. It takes a few minutes to slide the bags into the room and close the door. I flick the lock for good measure. Not that it will keep any of these alpha males from barging in if they choose.

I adjust my black leggings, as well as the soft tunic I slipped on since I knew we'd be traveling and climb onto the bed. It's more comfortable than the hotel room, like lying on a cloud.

Despite the events in Michail's bedroom, the distance between us now doesn't comfort me. I'm punishing him for making me feel guilty, for making me feel used. And a tiny part of me has to admit it wasn't all his fault. I pushed. He's the kind of man who pushes back. And when he pushes, things topple.

Why can't I stop thinking about him when I have an empire to retake? Not to mention my brother's wrath to deal with once he's done dude-broing it up with Michail. Despite my threat, if he tells Kai we did anything together, I might murder him. There are things I'd rather my all-seeing brother didn't know about me.

I roll on the bed, needing to take my mind off things. We are meeting up later to discuss planning, but for right now, I can reach out to my contacts, see if I can get some answers.

There are only a few people on my council I can contact safely. One of them being Maria, a lower member of the council with high ambitions. Not so high that she'd betray the only other woman on the council. When I took my seat, we agreed on solidarity. She'd help me, and I'd help her in return one day.

I dial her number, barely remembering it without my extensive contact list, and wait for her to answer.

"Come on," I mutter while I wait. If I get some answers, maybe I can get out from under the thumb of all these men intent on protecting me. I'm happy to keep my life, but the testosterone fest is grating on my nerves. One order after another, one move, one outfit, one smile...all to keep me safe, and all guaranteed to make me want to punch someone if they keep it up.

A tiny voice whispers that it's my fault. I'm the one who called Kai for help. This is his version of helping. Even Michail, in all his beautiful brooding, feels like he's suffocating me. Especially when he plays hot and cold with his body and emotions.

But how do I extricate myself without seeming ungrateful? I don't want to burn the bridges between my brother and me. Not since we are somewhat speaking again.

The phone cuts to a generic voicemail message, and I hang up. I grab the nearest pillow, press it over my face, and groan into it until all the air leaves my lungs.

"If you're trying to suffocate yourself, let me know. I'm happy to give you a hand. Just this once, of course," a voice says.

I glance up to find Kai leaning his hip against the footboard of the bed. Michail didn't follow him in, and I don't want to consider why that causes my chest to ache.

It's pointless to argue when Kai gets on a roll, so I keep still and wait for him to start and end his looming tirade.

Three...two...one...

"What the hell were you thinking? Or rather, you weren't thinking. Why would you agree to marry that asshole?"

I sit up and glare. "You mean the asshole who saved your life, and your girlfriend's life, so I've heard."

He slides onto the end of the bed, unbuttoning his suit jacket as he moves. "That has nothing to do with this. You aren't the one who has to pay my debts. I can cover them on my own."

I scoff. "This has nothing to do with you. Not everything does. This is about keeping myself safe and my seat secure."

He shifts his eyes to mine, his mouth still clamped in a grim line. "Is that what you really want? To marry a stranger, one who doesn't deserve you even at your brattiest, and run a corrupt office that is little more than window dressing in today's world?"

I can't explain to him how this is all I've ever known. This is what I've been trained for. The only thing I know how to do. If I lose my council seat, I have nothing and no reason to keep going. With Emmanuelle, I'll help run two councils. It will make me more powerful than anyone else in our society. In any city.

I might not hack things like Kai or kill things like Julia...but this...accumulating power...is something I can do, something I can control.

It doesn't matter. Kai can never understand. He's a man in this world. No one asks him to prove he deserves his place here.

"If that's all, I'm taking a nap." He shifts closer, opening his mouth, and I hold up my hand. "No, you have zero say in my relationships. You have zero control over my life. If I had known how this would go, I would have taken my chances on my own after the attack."

His jaw tightens, and his hands clench on his thighs. "We

protected you. Michail protected you. How can you say that? How can you be so ungrateful?"

I don't go into detail about how Michail protected me. Neither of us need to deal with that drama. "I meant what I said."

Kai stands, shoots me a withering look, and walks out of the room, slamming the door behind him.

The soft bed cradles me as I throw myself back. It grows dark outside the windows before I roll on my side and stare across the darkened room. Something feels like it's missing, and I hate it. A hot tear glides down my cheek, and I don't bother wiping it away.

I doze, then wake when warm skin touches my cheek. The scent of him tells me exactly who is touching me. I open my eyes and look up at him. It's dark, but I see his outline.

Without a word, he strips his jacket and shoes to climb into the bed. When he eases behind me and wraps me in his arms, I let him pull me into his chest and cradle me there in his warmth.

I don't allow people to comfort me. It leads to reliance, something I also never allow. But a few minutes of solidarity, I can handle. At least until I get a hold of myself and can face every demon lurking in this penthouse at once.

"Are you okay?" he whispers, as if he doesn't want to speak too loudly and scare me into not answering.

"My brother had a few things to say about my decision-making skills. I think he's not talking to me now. Which is pretty much par for the course."

He lifts one hand off my hips and brushes my cheek with his fingers. "What else is wrong?"

Do I tell him my body is still throbbing for him? Do I tell him I miss my home and the couple of people I consider a friend? I miss my family, and my house, and curling up with ice cream on a Friday night to watch reality TV. I miss my routine. Most of all, I miss this man's biting words and bossy tone. I'm sure as hell not admitting that to him.

His arms tighten around me and let our bodies mold together. Every inch of us is touching and reminding me of all the ways he's touched me since the moment we met.

Instead of answering his question, I deflect. "Why are you being so nice to me? I'm not telling my brother about what happened between us."

His tone takes on a defensive edge. "I can be nice."

I choose not to remind him of all the times he was decidedly not nice. "You can be nice if whatever act you have going on requires it."

He stiffens behind me, and I latch on to his wrists near my belly button, fearing he'll leave too soon.

"If we are throwing around accusations, you are even less nice than I am."

I stifle a chuckle. "I never claimed to be nice. In fact, I've made it my mission to be as unpleasant to you as possible."

"Mission accomplished then." There's a whisper of humor in his tone, and I can't help but smile.

His phone dings loudly, interrupting the moment. He checks it and mutters, "Kai," like a curse.

My brother's name is enough to make me pull away. "You better go. I'm sure you have new damsels to look after. Other people to torment."

Even in the dark, I can read the confusion on his face. The way his eyes scan my features looking for the truth, or the joke.

It's time to end this. Cut it off now before it hurts too much in the future. I never let my attachments go on long enough to hurt. "Besides, my fiancé will keep me safe from now on, once I get out of here."

My barb hits home. He slides off the bed and doesn't bother looking back at me before slamming the door behind him.

His leaving digs into my chest, a sharp ache to match the languorous one pulsing through my body from his touch. It'll ebb in time, and the more distance I can get, the better.

I hop off the edge of the bed, dig through my bags to consolidate, and pin down the one I'll need to get out of here and back to my life.

I can't keep living like this, especially with my brother thinking I'll stay under his thumb.

I dig my phone out of the blankets and use the browser to make some arrangements.

It's too soon to seek my fiancé's protection, and too late to go to Michail. It's time to do this on my own.

19

MICHAIL

She pushed me away, so I went. Even seeing through her words, I go, because she wants me to. Which doesn't explain why sneaks out of her room in the early morning hours and I simply allow it.

I know damn well she's not racing off to marry Emmanuelle, so what is she up to? Either way, I can't leave her to her own devices, not when she's determined to meet the business end of a gun if she keeps racing off like an idiot.

I'm good at following people, and she's not exactly hiding as she lugs one big bag down the stairwell and out the fire door leading to the garage attached to the building. I wait for her to get some distance and follow into the garage.

She hops into the back of an SUV, and I rush to my own sedate black two door. It's not fancy since fancy isn't great for keeping tabs on people. Fancy draws more attention than I like. Besides, I have better toys deeper in the garage.

I follow her vehicle through traffic, and I take way too long to realize we've started the lengthy drive to Chicago. It's a good thing I always keep my tank filled, or I would have lost her on the road.

I park a few cars down from her townhouse, where she stops and climbs out. The SUV heads off without her, and I curse her idiocy as she races up her brownstone steps without even looking around for danger.

I'm exhausted from the drive, flexing my hands on the steering wheel, trying to stir life into my extremities.

Even if no one comes for her tonight, she *will* answer to me. Answer to why she is putting herself in danger so recklessly. Hot molten anger leaks inside me, adding fire, burning hotter.

I climb out of the car and cross the street in the dark. It's still early in the morning, four by my phone clock.

Kai has texted me ten times, and I shut off the phone and tuck it into my pocket. I'll answer to him, same as she will face me first.

I amble closer to her home, keeping my eyes on the shadows, waiting for someone to make a move. I can feel it will happen. After years of chasing down danger, I have a good sense when it's nearby.

I glimpse a shiny gun in an overhead streetlight, and pick up my pace, keeping my steps light and quiet. She'll be tired, unprepared for an attack. The perfect moment for her enemies to catch her unaware.

If they don't murder her for arrogance, I might.

I stalk the man into the alley around the row of houses, keeping him in my sight, even as the shadows threaten to swallow him up.

He shimmies the lock on the backdoor with some kind of tool. I usually just use my boot, but I suppose he wants to make a quieter entrance. My victims usually know I'm coming.

He closes the door behind him, a considerate gesture since he's going to try to murder my girl.

My girl.

Well, my girl to protect at least.

I keep telling myself that as I slip into the house after the man and lock the deadbolt behind me. Something that should have already been done.

He moves silently, a professional, no doubt. But no one is as good as I am. As any of the Five are.

I creep behind him in the dark, using the streetlights from outside to guide my path. The downstairs is empty and quiet. He goes upstairs, one careful step up at a time.

I keep my mind on the intruder and not Selena and what she might be doing, what this man might catch her in the middle of. I'll allow him to get close enough before I kill him. Maybe it will give us a chance to learn who is behind this. Give us an edge.

As I sneak through the dark, I have to come to terms with the fact that I'm willing to put her up as bait to gain some answers. Hopefully, she understands the necessity. Even if she doesn't, I don't have time to ask.

The sound of her moving around comes from the only lit doorway at the end of the hall. The man slinks along the hallway until he stops at the door and pulls his gun from the holster under his black jacket.

Two can play this game, except I don't pull out a gun. I grab a knife from the sheath at my ankle. It's small but deadly and sharp. It'll do the job perfectly.

The man slowly opens the door, and I hold my breath as light spills down the hall to illuminate me. But he doesn't look back, cocky bastard.

I creep up on him as he enters the room. When he stops, I slip in behind him and watch as he holds the gun to the back of her head.

She freezes in stripping the clothing out of her suitcase.

I grind my teeth at the thought of him killing her here, her back to him. He won't even show her the courtesy of looking her in the eye when he kills her. What a prick.

I inch closer, not wanting to move too fast and spin the air around him, alerting him to my presence.

Selena keeps still, waiting. "If you're going to kill me, just get it over with."

The man jabs the gun into her head. "All in good time, baby. Look at you. I think I might play first. The boss won't mind as long as I finish the job when it's over."

Selena shifts and stands, her hands up, then turns to face him. She tenses when she sees me but doesn't betray my advantage with a stray look. "If you think I'll be an easy victim, you are dumber than you look."

The man traces the gun down her neck into her cleavage.

A red haze covers my vision, and it's like running, screaming down a long, dark tunnel. All I can see is this bastard touching what is mine. She won't die from his perversions yet, but he's hurting her, touching her, and I want his blood on my hands.

I step up behind him, wrap my arm around his neck in a lightning strike, and sink the blade into his flesh. It takes seconds to reduce him to a sputtering stain on her carpet, his blood sprayed across my arm and Selena, who stood in front of him.

She lowers her trembling hands, staring at me, no doubt seeing the side I've kept carefully hidden. The monster under the masks.

"You...you" she sputters.

She sees me now, but it's too late. She's the prey I didn't even know I hunted. I drop the bloody knife to the floor and step over the dead bastard, still bleeding out. "What the fuck were you thinking coming back here? Do you have any sense of self-preservation?"

A spark of anger lights her eyes like a candle in a dark window. "You can't blame this on me."

I point at the man on the floor. "You think he was here for me? He sat outside waiting, no doubt for weeks, watching until you returned so he could finish the job someone else started."

She dips her eyes to the body and back to me. "You saved me."

I crowd her, pushing her back into a tall dresser until she can't escape. "This time, I did. But what if I wasn't here? You'd be dead right now, or worse."

She shoves at my chest, trying to push me away, and then reaches behind her to jerk a gun from the waistband of her pants. "Back up, I get enough lectures from my brother. I don't need them from you too."

"You didn't think to pull this out when he caught you unaware?"

She scoffs. "I let him catch me. I left the door unlocked. Hell, I practically invited the bastard into my house. I hoped to get some answers. Maybe he'd spill something in all his posturing and threats. I would never have let him touch me."

I grab her wrist, twisting it until the gun slips out of her hand to clatter on the floor. "Don't point a gun at me. He has friends outside too. What were you planning for them?"

She hikes her chin up, challenging when she should back down. She does not know how close I am to ripping her apart. "I would have dealt with that too."

I kick her knees out and let her land hard on the floor, her legs instantly soaking up her assailant's blood.

She tries to break the hold I have on her neck but doesn't succeed.

"Look at him," I growl. "Is this what you wanted? You want me to drag the others up here and slaughter every single one of them for you? Is that what this is?"

She shivers and says nothing.

"You think you're the smartest person in the room, and you don't even realize how big that room is. You can never be the smartest. You can never be the fastest." I kneel beside her and force her to meet my eyes. "I'm not saying you aren't smart. I'm saying your arrogance is a flaw people will learn to exploit. It's how they took your council seat so easily."

She wiggles, trying to get free again, but I've had enough of this spoiled brat and her ego. It's time to teach her once and for all that she belongs to me, and I protect what's mine.

I drag her up by the back of her neck and spin her into my chest. "You are such a brat, but guess what? I just saved your life. Time to pay the fucking tab."

20

SELENA

I stare up at him, no doubt looking as lost as I feel right now. Some of the anger has cooled, and I shift my gaze to see the blood pool from his victim inch closer to my bare feet. "I should clean up the carpet." I wave at the mess encroaching on my personal space, but he gives me a shake, his fingers digging into my biceps.

"What the fuck? Don't worry about the body. I have people for that. He tried to kill you and talked about raping you. He deserves what he got." He's tilting his head this way and that, as if studying every angle of my face. Maybe in the shock, he can't read me like he usually does. This isn't the first time I've seen a dead body, but it is the first time I can feel the stickiness congealing against my bare toes. No one is immune to something like that.

I drag my eyes from the pool of blood and look at his face again. His jaw is tense, his eyebrows drawn up tight. Despite his original outburst, he hasn't dragged me to the bed by the hair yet. I guess I should be thankful he hasn't given in to his caveman brain, at least any more than he already has.

"Why are you looking at me like that?" he asks, his voice dipping low.

I clear my throat. "Like what? I'm just looking at you. You're the one who declared I need to pay up...so..."

His eyes narrow, and his full lips thin even further. "This is not the time to challenge me."

When I made this plan, I knew someone would likely die, and I simply hoped it wasn't me. Now, all I can think about is the dead man on my floor and how his blood will stain everything. Why does it matter to me? This man meant to murder me, so it really shouldn't.

Michail keeps his eyes locked on my face and digs his phone out of his suit jacket. "Don't move while I get one of my cleaners out here. We aren't finished talking about this."

I try to clear my features to keep him from seeing more than I want him to right now. I feel like an exposed nerve two seconds away from the wrong thump.

He steps away and whispers into his phone. It takes work, but I keep my gaze off the dead man and on Michail instead. Any second he'll pounce, and I'm not ready for whatever he'll demand from me.

Someone says my name. It sounds far away and muffled.

"Selena!"

I blink and look up to find Michail in front of me again. The anger has slipped out of his features, leaving something which looks vaguely like concern behind.

"Yes?" I ask, hoping he didn't ask me something. All I think I heard is my name.

He reaches up to brush his thumb along my cheek. "Do what you need to do. Put on the mask if it makes things go away for a while."

His words make sense, and I'm not in the best place to argue about the mental health of his proposition. I close my eyes, ground myself in his touch. Here in this moment, there's a mask I haven't put on, one some part of me is longing to wear.

I let his thumb continue its swipe over my cheek and relax into his grasp. "I need to take a shower and get out of these clothes so your friend can take them when he leaves with the body."

He glances down at his own suit. "You're right. You must be doing better than I thought."

There's a note of humor in his tone, but it's testing, teasing. When I don't match the lightness in his voice, he takes off his clothes one piece at a time. There's nothing slow or sexy about it, but my mouth goes dry with every bit of his skin revealed.

I scan down his body, cataloging each scar, each freckle. His muscles flex as he kicks the last of his clothing away and waits for me to follow suit.

I'm not a self-conscious person. I only hesitate because I want to stare at him a little longer. He grows impatient and grabs the hem of my shirt and rips it over my head. My ponytail slaps back against my bare skin when he tosses the clothing away.

I scowl and swat at his next attempt to grab me. "I can do it myself. I don't need you to undress me."

Keeping my eyes off the crimson pool, I strip the rest of my blood-stained clothing and let them fall into the pile at Michail's feet.

When I finish and look at him, his gaze is locked on my body, his eyes roaming from my hips to my breasts, and back down again.

So I don't say anything stupid. I clamp my lips together and let him grab my hand. He leads me into the bathroom, opens the shower stall, and flips the faucets on. I barely wait for the water to warm before climbing in. He joins me, leaving more than enough room around us. My shower could host an orgy if I were so inclined.

Under the spray, I turn my back, but his rough hands curl around my waist before I even have time to get my hair properly wet. He spins me to face him, crowding close. "We weren't done with our conversation. What were you thinking coming back here with a half-cocked plan and no way to defend yourself?"

I grit my teeth and glare up at him since he's trapped me against the onyx tile with his body. "You saw my gun. I was perfectly capable of taking care of myself. I never invited you here, and you've made it clear at every turn that you think I'm a useless, spoiled brat."

The edge of his lip twitches like he might smile. If he does, I might punch him in the throat. "You don't know a thing about what's going on in my head, but for the record, I do think you're a spoiled brat."

It doesn't escape me he neglected to add useless to his accusation. The omission registers, but not in time for me to stop my hand from connecting with his cheek.

He sucks in a loud, long breath, and another. My fingers ache a little from the contact as guilt slithers along my sternum down to my gut.

"You raise a hand to me again, and I'll make you pay for it," he grits between his teeth. "You being a spoiled brat is practically your brand. Something I didn't think you were ashamed of until right this second."

I wrap my arms over my breasts, hiding my body. We are not having this conversation right now while we are both naked.

He jerks my loofah from a hook, glares at me, and adds soap to it. I'm about to ask what he's doing when he uses it on me. Spreading the lather over my shoulder, down my arm, then prying my hand loose to wash my breasts.

"What are you doing?" It's a dumb question, but I can't help it. Why is he washing my body when I slapped him? When I've called him names, pushed him away, and done everything possible to make his life miserable?

I swat at his hands, trying to keep them off me. "Stop it. I can wash my body. Just leave me alone."

It's so much easier to push them all away. The second I allow anyone in, they take advantage. Every single person, save my family, has betrayed me in some way. They see me as a commodity. My body, my position, my power. It's all to buy, sell, or trade.

Men think if they can gain my heart, I'll give them anything. Women think if they can gain my trust, I'll give them everything.

There are maybe a handful of people I actually trust, and with the way Michail looks at me, I can't allow him to join that list. Not when I already want him to take all of me.

To keep all of me. For once in my life, I don't want to be alone, and yet I have no frame of reference for what such a thing even looks like.

The water at our feet is faintly pink, and the second I notice the color, my knees wobble. Michail scoops me against him, and I gasp. There's something carnal about two wet, slick bodies sliding along each other. And Michail has a lot of muscle and height to rub up against.

"Just leave me alone," I try again.

He ignores me and uses his soapy loofah to scrub down my back, then around to my ass, and finally to my legs. Once every inch of me is soaped up, he steps back enough to stand under the other shower head and gives himself a cursory scrub.

I reach for my hair, spreading it out so I can wash it. It's been a few days, and I'd hate it if I found blood in it later.

He doesn't allow me to wash my hair either. All I can do is stand and huff while he scrubs at my scalp with his strong fingers. Damn it, why does he have to be so good at practically everything?

When every bit of me is clean, he pushes me into the tile wall again. The steam has heated it, but I can't help but shiver at a few chilled bits of stone.

"Talk to me," he says, his eyes roving over my bare flesh still, never up to my eyes.

"What do you want me to say? What will it take to get you to let me out of this shower so I can take care of myself?"

He shakes his head. "Not a damn thing. The cleaner is out there, and I won't allow another man to see you naked."

My stomach does a flip-flop at the way he says it. The sheer arrogance of his tone lights me up. This is a man who goes after what he wants, and for some reason, he's decided to want me, even if it's such a bad idea.

"Oh, yeah? And if I walk out there right now?" It's a challenge, and nothing more. I don't want some random stranger to see me naked any more than he does.

But his voice is soft and deadly serious as he answers. "I'll put a bullet into his brain and anyone else dumb enough to look."

It takes me a second to assimilate that he is serious. He'd kill someone for looking at me. Where was this man when he wanted sucked off under the table, or when he might have fucked me on a random office desk? What's changed to make him think I belong to him?

"You don't control me. The only reason I'm not kicking you out of my house right now is because you're pretty to look at. Don't, for a second, think that I've got feelings for you."

Fuck. The venom I use to keep others away poured out of me before I could reel it back in. It has to be the shock from the fresh attack and the sheer domination in Michail's gaze as he stares at me. Men have coveted me before, but I've never wanted them to succeed in taking me. Not like I want Michail too. Even in his dominance, he's beautiful, or maybe he's beautiful for his dominance. I don't allow myself to consider it too closely. Not when the heat in his eyes fizzles, while every part of me still burns.

His jaw clenches, and I can hear his teeth grinding together over the shower spray. "You think I'm just another pretty face, huh? Maybe you are just like all those other council bitches, then. Here I'd thought you were different."

A rush of heady fear sweeps through my heated veins at the edge in his voice now. When I open my mouth to speak, he clamps his hand across my lips. "No, don't talk. I'm not here for conversation, am I? We both know I'm only here to look pretty and lick your cunt good enough that you can crawl back to your fiancé and take his dick. So that you, and he, can forget for a little while that you don't loathe each other."

There's something dark and far away in his gaze. Did I push him too far?

"Michail?" I mumble against his palm.

But it's no use. He doesn't even see me now. He's gone somewhere else, somewhere deep inside himself. I don't know if I can reach him there, not when I caused this.

Fuck. Why did I have to open my mouth? Why can't I just fucking let shit happen for once and stop fighting back so hard, especially against things I actually want?

He slides his hand sideways, still at the same pressure until he slaps the wet tile with a loud twack. "So what will it be this time? Do you want me on my knees or are you going to sit on my face?"

As appealing as both options sound, I shake my head. "No, stop. This isn't what I want."

His voice is barely audible when he says, "I guess you should have thought about that before you touched me."

21

MICHAIL

It's as if something clicked in my brain. A switch, a trigger, waiting for the proper pressure. Selena is safety and ruin in one sinful package. She's everything I want in a woman, and yet I can't stop the words which pour from my lips.

She's not them.

She didn't use my body and discard me to go back to her husband. She didn't sell me into slavery to watch me dangle.

I try to gain control again, slow things down, but my pulse is turning my cock to stone, and I can already taste her on my tongue like the worst craving.

"What will it be?" I repeat, hating every angry syllable dripping out of my mouth.

She glares up at me, her back plastered to the wall, her tits rising and falling with every strangled, angry breath. "How about neither? You walk out of this shower and go back to your lonely life."

I bark out a laugh, and it echoes in the enclosed shower. A mocking sound. Fitting. "Not going to happen, Princess. You're the one who says you don't have feelings for me. Prove it. Use me like I know you want to."

I spear my fingers into her body without warning. Her hands wrap around my wrist to pull me off, but she's not strong enough to move me unless I want to be moved. "Just as I expected. You're soaked, and so ready, I could slide into you right now."

She swallows so hard I can see her throat working. "Stop it. Don't do this. Not like this." Her voice is barely a whisper, as if she can't allow anyone to hear her plead at full volume. "If you do this, you can't take it back. Not for either of us."

I narrow my eyes and lean in, so she doesn't miss the ice infiltrating my gaze despite the steamy shower. "You're the one who called me a pretty decoration. Useless for anything but fucking, right?"

"You're twisting my words. Stop it."

I pull my fingers from her body and bring them to my mouth to lick them clean. Perfect. She tastes just as perfect as I remember.

She's right. I am twisting her words. But it's to remind myself that she's part of the world which so cruelly turned me into the monster I am today. Along the way, I'd forgotten that simple fact. I can't allow myself to forget again.

In what I assume is a last-ditch effort to pull me back, she rises to her tiptoes and presses her forehead to mine. "Michail, please. Fuck me instead. Don't let the past ruin whatever this is, even if it doesn't extend beyond tonight. Don't let them win."

I brace my hands on the wall alongside her head and breathe. Not because I fear I'll hurt her, but because I fear I'll say something I can't take back.

Words tumble through my mind. How beautiful she is, how sexy she is, how much I want to claim every inch of her body with my teeth. I can't say a single thing for fear that she really is just like the rest of them. She never claimed to be any different.

I dip my chin and kiss her hard, using my tongue and teeth to coax her mouth open underneath mine. She doesn't put up a fight, letting me take control and plunder her mouth until she's panting.

When I pull away again, we are both breathing heavily. "Do you know why I'm a virgin?"

Usually, she'd have some smart, mocking crack, but now she only shakes her head and shrugs lightly, waiting for me to tell her what I obviously want to reveal.

"Those bitches didn't want to get pregnant, but they also didn't want to use a condom. So they agreed amongst themselves to ride my face as often as they wanted, but they wouldn't fuck me, and I couldn't find someone else to do it for me. Not when I'd been locked up more than I'd been free."

She's breathing harder now, her entire chest rising and falling heavily. But she doesn't speak. No words of encouragement to keep speaking, and no words of forgiveness, loyalty, or love. Nothing but silence.

At that moment, I know silence is fine. I can live with silence if it means I can have her, even for one night.

I turn the faucet to cut the water, my eyes never leaving hers. Then I scoop her up into my arms and carry her out of the stall. The clean up better be done by now, or there are going to be a lot more bodies to take care of.

Her room is empty when I enter, and the alarm panel blinks from beside the door. Good. No interruptions.

I snag a couple of towels, stand her beside the bed, and go to work on drying her from head to toe. When every inch of her pale skin is rosy and dry, I lift her onto the bed and quickly swipe a towel over myself.

She watches with wide eyes, her gaze drifting down my abs to my cock, and back to my face every so often.

I toss the towels away and climb up on the bed with her, slowly invading her space so she has no choice but to lie back on the pillows and part her warm thighs.

"You have no idea how often I've imagined what this would feel like. Both of us are completely naked, my dick perfectly lined up with your pussy."

She nods frantically. "Me too. I've imagined it too."

I nibble a trail up her neck. "When?"

Her fingers dig into my hair, holding me against her. "Always, all the damn time. You drive me insane, Michail."

I bite her shoulder and sit back, enjoying the way my mark looks on her skin. "Say it again."

Her eyes are closed, her head thrown back. "Michail."

She could have feigned ignorance, but she knew exactly what I wanted. I lift off her enough to reach between our bodies and squeeze the head of my dick. At this rate, I'll blow before I even get inside her, and I won't allow that.

Hesitantly, she curls her hands around my neck and tugs me back on top of her. Off balance, I drop my weight, and she wraps her legs around my hips to keep me trapped. "You're mine now," she whispers against my mouth.

"Fine," I answer back. "Then you belong to me too. You're fucking mine."

Neither of us wants to be claimed by another person, but in this stalemate, it's the only option, or else we'll consume each other.

We stare into each other's eyes, both of us testing the weight of this claim. "I want that bastard's ring off your finger immediately. He has zero claim on you now."

She nods. "He never did. I would never sleep with him."

I restrain a retort because I don't want to fight, not for real. She's stolen the fight in me during our shower, tossing it away with soft-spoken words and tender touches. It curbed the anger long enough to come back to myself before I did something stupid. Before I ruined things between us forever. I have no doubt she'd have let me continue, play out whatever sick fantasy I'd built up in my head for revenge, but it would have broken things between us irrevocably.

I reach between us again, angling my hips so I can slide my hand, palm down, over her thigh. She arches into my touch when my fingertips graze her pussy. Fucking hell, she always feels so damn hot and wet when I touch her.

I circle her clit gently, coaxing every huff and gasp I'm able from her lips. As she reaches the edge of her orgasm, I stop, withdrawing to wait.

Her eyes fly open, her gaze flint and fire. "Are you fucking kidding me? You can't tease me like that."

I shift my hips again, this time finding the right angle, the one I need to slide my cock along the seam of her. The second the head of me rubs over her clit, she arches off the bed, an almost whine escaping her lips.

"Why does that feel so good?" she complains, her eyes squeezed tight.

It's a good question. I want to slide inside that heat and fuck her into the mattress, but the rational part of me continues to take things slow. To let her get used to the feel of me.

When the teasing becomes too much for even me, I guide my cock to her opening and carefully feed my body inside hers. She clenches, her cunt sucking me in with such a tight grasp, I fear I'll come before I'm fully seated.

"Relax, Princess. Relax for me." Both an order and a plea. Fuck. Every slight movement pushes me closer. But I want more than a quick blow out. I want to take my time with her. Remember this moment, the moment she chose *me*.

She sags against the bed, but it does nothing to ease the grip of her body on mine. Her forehead bunches, and I slow, waiting for her expression to clear again. When she relaxes more, I continue, maintaining my steady pace until I'm flat against her.

Nothing has ever felt this good, except maybe the feel of her silken mouth around me. "Are you alright?" I whisper against her temple.

She forces a breath through her nose and nods. "I'm fine. See, I told you I'd be gentle with you for your first time."

I roll my eyes and swivel my hips. We both gasp at the sensation, and then I have to move.

My brain is demanding I claim her, mark her, ensure the world knows she belongs to me. Her nails dig into my shoulders, and I let myself believe she feels the same need to mark me as hers.

I ease out of her incrementally and then glide back in. Each sensation is different. When we have time, I'll explore them all with her.

Her nails carve down my back to rest against my ass. "Will you stop teasing me and fuck me?"

I stop, pressing my weight off her so I can see her face better. "You could say please."

She narrows her eyes and digs her nails in harder. "Will you fuck me, please?"

I duck my head and kiss her hard. "That's my girl."

Then I let myself go. I release myself to the feeling, allowing whatever movement, action, or direction feels good. Soon, I'm slamming into her, and she's raising her hips to meet me. Every single one of my nerve endings feels like it's on fire, and I'd rather burn for eternity than stop.

She comes first, and I can't help the groan of satisfaction that rushes out of me. I fucking did that. No one else will make her come like that except me.

Her cunt clenches in a rhythm I try to match with each thrust, and all too soon, my balls are tight, and I fall over the cliff myself. One minute I'm coming, and the next, I'm staring down at her like I blacked out for a second. The rush of sensation crashes into me, obliterating any hope I had of letting her go again.

She scans my features. "Are you okay?"

I nod and press off her to roll onto my side. Fluid follows me out of the hold of her body, and I glance down to make sure she's ok. Red smears over her thighs, and I test it with my finger.

Blood. There's blood mixed with my cum, and I shift to look at her face. It's red from the fucking, but there's a telltale patch high on her cheekbones when she blushes.

"I guess I should have told you I was a virgin too," she whispers.

I roll on my side to look at her easier. "What? How is that possible? I could have sworn you rubbed my nose in being a virgin."

She rolls to mirror me, curling her knees up between us. "So what? I'm sure you've learned I'm a smart-off-now-think-about-the-consequences-later kind of girl."

"Why did you wait so long?"

She doesn't meet my eyes when she says, "I couldn't let anyone have that sort of power over me."

The air stirs, and she hops to the side of the bed to throw me a look over her shoulder. It contains none of the warmth we just shared. "So we're all paid up, right? You should go."

22

SELENA

After I rip my own heart out, I retreat to the bathroom and clean myself up. I take longer than usual hoping he's gone before I exit again.

Once my teeth are brushed, my hair is braided, and I've found a clean pajama set, I open the bathroom door.

An exhale rushes out of me, and I cross the room to check the alarm. It's set, which means he knows my code, or he simply left my room and not the house entirely. But that minor dilemma is something to consider tomorrow.

I crawl into bed and shuffle the covers around. Even though we both showered beforehand, I still catch notes of lemongrass wafting from the bedding.

It's enough to lull me to sleep. Not enough to ensure I actually get a good night's sleep.

I wake in the morning feeling stiff, sore, and all around grumpy as fuck. There is no alarm to set, no early morning meeting, so I don't bother getting out of bed. Why should I when I've built my world up to this moment? The very moment I realize I'm sitting on my throne all by myself. I'll never be able to trust anyone to sit beside me there.

I'll never be able to trust anyone with the burdens of power I usually wish away.

When sunlight peaks through the curtains, I get up and head for my closet. There are only a few gaps in my wardrobe, specifically things I packed to take with when Michail carted me off. I'll have to get the pieces cleaned and added back into my rotation where they belong.

The simple act of organizing what's been out of place, of reclaiming my home, is enough to calm the chatter in my head. At least for a little while.

It's not until I'm sitting alone at my countertop, the house quiet and empty around me, that a slight tremor rolls through me. It threatens to break me open like a hollow chocolate bunny in a toddler's grasp.

Even if this is my decision, I have to live with the consequences. Not touching Michail again is one big fucking consequence I haven't resigned myself to yet. And if we do cross paths again, I should fear his retribution. His revenge. No doubt he's added me to his list after my performance last night.

His words from last night echo in my head. *Put on the mask if it makes things go away for a while.*

It's a simple thing, something I can do to soothe the raw edges of my nerves. Of the gaping hole where my heart is.

Somehow, in all the fear, pain, and anger... I fell in love with Michail. I'll never breathe a word of it, since it would put us both in danger, but I'm a little stunned at the revelation. I've never been in love...not like this. Being in lust is an entirely different creature, something I've had lots of practice with.

I shove down my breakfast and head to my office to find my phone. When I sit behind my desk, I sigh softly. It feels like it's been forever since I sat here and did actual work. Took care of the society I swore myself to uphold. Not that there is much to uphold amongst criminals. But that's the point...someone has to keep the masses from going too far. From tipping attention in our favor.

I'm good at my job, and it's time to remind everyone why.

I find the contact I need and hit the dial button. She's the same woman I called the other day and only reached the voicemail. Every contact goes the same way. No one answers, and I'm sent to generic voice mails all around.

On the last one, I squeeze the phone a little too tight and respond. "Spread the word. I've returned to Chicago, and nothing is driving me away this time. If you're one of my allies, then you better prepare yourself. If you're one of my enemies, I offer the same advice."

When I finish my calls, I check my email. There's nothing since the initial attack. How could no one need me all this time?

I scroll through the email to reach the trash folder and uncover email after email. All responded to, but definitely not by me. This is my official email address, not personal, so whomever has deigned to assume my seat on the council has used it. Where did they get the password?

I spend hours combing the emails for even a hint of who has overthrown me. Nothing pops out. When I stand, the light in the room is waning, and I shuffle toward the kitchen to eat so I can go up to bed.

My gun is sitting on the counter when I enter, making me freeze, my hand still on the light switch.

I don't see him so much as feel him. He shifts from the couch in the living room, his eyes on me, even though I can't meet them through the darkness in that room. "What are you doing here?'

His tone is clipped and clawed and curtained. There's absolutely no give. "My job."

Two words which stab into my gut, threatening to send me to my knees. I manage a throaty, "Oh."

Suddenly, I'm not so hungry. I snatch the gun from the counter, check the rounds, flip the light off again, and make my way back to my bedroom. If I were smart, I'd escape the scent of him by sleeping in one of the guest rooms, but something in me can't resist allowing the scent of him to curl around me while I sleep. The day I no longer smell him might kill me. For now, I deal the best way I know how, in a world I created myself.

I climb into the bed, snuggle under the covers, and pretend I'm not crying.

When he climbs into bed beside me, I pretend I didn't scoot over to make room. I pretend his arms around me mean absolutely nothing.

I slip into the mask even if a void is opening inside me underneath it.

23

MICHAIL

I leave her bed early. Neither of us can deal with waking up beside each other right now. And likely never will.

My bag sits on the perfectly made bed in one of her guest rooms. I pull out some underwear, shower quickly, and don one of the suits I stashed in the walk-in closet. She told me to leave, but I refuse to go until I know she's safe. Back here, headfirst in the pit of snakes, is the opposite of safe.

She doesn't understand that I can't leave her to her fate, even if she's made it clear she doesn't want or need me.

I grab a protein bar from her pantry and sit on the couch to check progress emails from the team on my tablet. When she finally graces the world with her presence, she looks immaculate, as usual. But a little more dressed up than I've seen her recently.

"Where are you going?"

She doesn't spare me a glance as she rifles through her refrigerator. "Lunch with a friend."

"Which friend?"

This time she turns to look at me. "That is none of your business."

I stand and drop my tablet onto the nearest pillow. She takes a few retreating steps when I stalk into the kitchen. The tether of my patience snapped the night she shoved me out of her bed. "While I'm guarding you, everything you do is my business. Right now, you can't take a fucking shit without letting me know."

She wrinkles her nose. "Do you have to be so crass?"

I lean over the counter, my hands flat on the granite. "I'm the hired help, remember? The human fuck-toy. I'm always crass."

When it's time for her to leave for lunch, she holds the door open for me to exit first. We ride to the restaurant in silence, and I survey the small crowd as we squeeze through the tables to her friend.

She's dressed in a fussy female suit, her blonde hair sporting streaks of gray. I'd recognize the set of her shoulders anywhere. They inch higher, toward her ears, the closer she gets to orgasm. Margery Turner. Wife of oil tycoon Richard Turner, and one of my very first female clients when I turned sixteen. It seems like years ago now. The memories crowd in, but I keep my mask in place and let them pass by me.

When Selena sits, I take the other empty seat and study the newcomer's face carefully. It's been years since I've seen her. Years since I had to sell my body for protection. Years since Adrian plucked me from that life to give me a purpose.

A purpose and a promise that one day, I'll feel their blood on my hands.

She barely spares me a glance, and Selena is content to ignore my presence too. Usually, I'd call her on it, but I don't want to get into an argument in front of my old client. I don't want to give her a reason to remember.

Margery grasps Selena's hands over the menus. "I've missed you so, sweet child."

Selena scoffs. "You aren't even that much older than me. Don't call me that."

She puts on a pretty pout. "But I started with my council seat while your parents still ruled. I guess I will always see you as a child, somewhat."

Selena's eyes flash to me, but she keeps her features blank and surveys her menu, tucking her hands into her lap now that Margery is done playing the doting mother.

I've seen this act more times than I can count. Older woman, more experience, seducing someone younger to his or her ways. Margery wants something from Selena. Badly. Or else, why risk a meeting while death hangs over Selena's head?

What is in this for her?

I decide to find out. Not for any sense of loyalty toward Selena, but because the information could be useful later to the Five, or hell, even to me when the time comes to slit this woman's throat for all the atrocities she's committed.

I fall back into a mask I know well and have perfected over the years. Pasting on a dumb, pretty smile, I wait for Margery to glance my way. In a heartbeat I snare her, and she doesn't even know it yet.

"I'm Mich. I don't think we've been introduced."

She extends her hand almost shyly. With a gentle shake, I release her, careful not to wipe my hand on my pants to get rid of the feel of her.

"Margery, of course." She says it like I should have recognized her the moment we sat down. Well, I did, but not for whatever reason she expects.

Selena shoots me a glare, as if it will deter me. She's made me immune to those looks with how often she tosses them around.

I focus on Margery, my skin crawling. "I'm so sorry, but have we met before? I can't place you and feel so guilty for not remembering." I push a little southern drawl into my tone and let her melt all over.

"No, I don't believe so. I'd remember someone as beautiful as you."

It takes no effort to draw up an array of thoughts that force a blush into my cheeks. Let her think I'm sweet. That is her type, after all.

The server brings salad and bread for the table, then refills the drinks, and makes a hasty retreat.

Selena captures Margery's attention again, but I make sure when Margery glances my way, she sees a sweet smile and dopey empty eyes. An easy mark for her to lay claim to.

"Who do you think is behind this attack?" Selena asks her friend and fellow councilwoman.

Margery considers her salad and then shakes her head. "I don't know. No one has stepped up to claim ownership, and the others are worried. The society here in Chicago is worried. You need to take the throne, if even for one day, so you can reassure our people."

I narrow my eyes at the way she says "our people" like they belong to her in a way that doesn't completely fall under benevolence.

The women chat back and forth a little longer, forgoing dessert for a hot cup of coffee. I keep my attention equally split between them. The interaction has already given me more knowledge of how Selena's mind works. In fact, I can see now how much she wants this. How much her council seat means to her. It's not because she thinks it's her legacy. It's because she worked hard to earn her position and enjoys taking care of her people. How original. Many of the Five have learned the hard way that councilmembers can't be trusted. Not even Selena.

After the other night, especially Selena.

I settle into my chair, but it's not long before a hand squeezes my thigh.

One look between them, and it's easy to guess who thinks they have the right to touch me. Selena won't even look at me, let alone manhandle me.

Margery's hand slides higher to the inside of my thigh, almost to my crotch. It takes all my self-discipline to keep from squeezing her wrist, showing her the strength she is fucking with. I clamp her wrist gently and ease her hand off my lap. When she glances my way again, I give her a cute little frown and send my curls spinning with a little shake of my head.

When lunch is over, I'm ready to take a shower and fill my brain with anything that isn't the banal chitchat of this woman. Even the tone of her voice grates on me by the end.

She slips her card into my hand under the table and gives me a wink before leaving.

I turn my attention to Selena, sure she'd be looking anywhere but at me, except when my eyes reach hers, she's staring, and staring hard.

"What the fuck was that?"

I tuck Margery's card into my pocket above the table so Selena can see it. "What was what?"

She waves toward the door. "Why were you flirting with her? Oh, I apologize, was I supposed to flirt with you too? You didn't specify what my duties were before we arrived."

We glare at each other, and then she stifles a groan in her cupped hands. "How is this different from when we were at the casino? You called the shots then, but now it's my turn. You can leave anytime that becomes a problem for you."

"This is different because everything I did was to keep you safe."

Her eyes narrow to slits. "So fucking my face under the VIP room table was to keep me safe. Yeah, I get that. How about the numerous times you kissed me? Were all those to keep me safe too? You are so full of bullshit, Michail. You don't even know what the truth looks like anymore. Hell, I bet you don't even know the real you under all these masks...these acts."

Her barb hits home, but I don't allow her to see it. Anything I say right now will be laced with venom, so I will keep my mouth shut.

After a few moments of silence, she huffs and shakes her head. "Is it because you have a problem following the orders of a woman?"

"Why the fuck would that matter? I follow Valentina's orders all the time. She gets bossier and bossier by the day thanks to Adrian's influence. And something tells me your brother's intended won't shy away from a dictate or two when she's integrated with us more."

"So, you just don't want to follow *my* orders. Why?"

It's on the tip of my tongue to explain it to her. To lay out all the ways she belongs to me and all the ways I'm honored to protect her body and mind. But no, she doesn't want that. She made it clear I mean nothing more to her than a drugstore dildo.

The server brings her bill, she pays it quickly, and we leave the restaurant. It hits me when we climb into her SUV.

"You were jealous."

She scoffs, but it's not sincere. Not for a second. "What do I have to be jealous about? Margery has a husband she adores. Anything she does outside of her marriage is at her discretion, but she never gets attached."

I want to disillusion her. Explain how her friend didn't get attached to a sixteen-year-old sex slave she kept under lock and key for weeks. She has no idea who her enemies are because she doesn't even know her friends.

Which, considering how things went with us, I can't say I am surprised.

I keep quiet about Margery's secrets for now. Especially about the letter M carved into the back of my thigh. It's nothing more than a faint-white scarred outline now, but then, it was one scar too many. One more thing meant to break my will and my spirit.

We get back to Selena's house, and she tosses her keys onto her countertop. "There. We had a successful outing where no one tried to kill me, and neither of us killed each other." There's an edge to her tone, though, which says she's still considering the option.

I meet her eyes, and I can't look away. Not from her anger, from her pain, or her pleasure. She shows so much in her eyes, and she doesn't even realize it. Even under the masks, the acts, all of it, I can always read her eyes. I was too wrapped up in my pleasure the other night to read what she was about to do to me. And that is partially on me for not expecting to be blindsided.

The anger rears up anew, and I have to turn away from her to contain it.

"What?" she asks. "What was that look? This is your fault too. You're the one who demanded sexual favors for protection."

I head up to the guest room and close the door quietly. This is my fault.

Maybe when Kai finds out and kills me for touching her, I'll be free of it all.

It's not right now that hurts. It's the memories. Every single one a tiny needle digging into my skin, ready to be tugged, rearranged, and sunk deeper at any moment.

24

SELENA

Michail's presence has gone from distracting to all-consuming. It's late in the day, and I step out on my front stairs to watch the last of the sunset over the sliver of water view I have from here. It's lovely to watch, each individual ray adding to the symphony of color and light to create something beautiful and a little bit awe-inspiring.

I feel him before I see him, even before the air around me stirs when he throws himself onto the stone steps beside me. He doesn't offer a greeting, so I don't speak either.

But his entirely consuming presence makes it hard to stay alert to dangers—things like armed men firing weapons from their vehicles. I hear the first bullet pinging off the brick before I'm moving, never having seen the small red SUV which slows to a crawl as it passes my house.

Michail is faster than me. He curls around my front, throwing himself between me and the bullets, which is not better than getting shot myself. Why would he do that? Pulling me out of harm's way is one thing. Throwing himself in front of something that can easily kill him is another.

More gunfire causes him to grab my bicep, haul me to my feet, and race inside the house with me stumbling along beside him. With the door between us and the guns, I feel better. Still, we both hit the floor, pressing our bellies to the hardwood as we wait for the noise to end and the cars to finish their run.

Any non-society members on this street will have also called the police when the gunfire erupted, helping curtail the number of bullets we might be trying to dodge right now.

A soft knock draws both our attention. I shake my head, content to remain belly down in my foyer until I know it's safe.

Michail doesn't handle wait-and-see very well. He presses his long body off the floor in a feat of strength, then stands and opens the door, keeping himself behind the barrier of it.

It's not armed assailants coming to finish the job. It's Emmanuelle.

I shove off the floor this time too and straighten my dress. He enters, a soft smile on his lips, his hair coiffed, wearing a gold smoking jacket and shiny black shoes.

"Going out?"

He shrugs and offers me a small white box with a bow.

I risk a glance at Michail, who stands off to the side, his jaw wired shut, but his eyes shooting pointy objects at Emmanuelle's back.

Two more men, both in black-on-black suits, enter the house behind Emmanuelle and shut the door.

"Friends of yours?" I ask.

Emmanuelle glances over his shoulder and offers a winsome smile. "Sure, or bodyguards, if you prefer. I see yours is still around. We scared off your shooters out there but didn't see anything that might help you identify them."

I lead Emmanuelle into my sitting room, carefully placing his gift on the coffee table, and try not to look uncomfortable when he takes the love seat next to me, so close our thighs almost touch.

Michail takes the armchair across from us, and the two strangers stay by the front door.

Isn't this cozy?

I sigh and pin a smile in place. "So, what can I do for you?"

Emmanuelle tilts his head, regarding me with a mix of curiosity and exasperation. Like I did something cute he hasn't quite come to terms with yet. "You've returned home, so I assume we should get on with our plans. I wanted to come sooner, but I had business overseas. Now, as for what else I'm doing here, I brought you an invitation. One you might be particularly interested in since you usually host it."

It takes me way too long to figure out what he means. "They are holding the charity ball this year?" I haven't gotten an invite, and even with several attempts on my life, being excluded hurts so much more. I can't believe they didn't invite me.

Emmanuelle reaches out and presses my chin up so he can look into my eyes. I resist jerking my face from his touch. I need him to play a specific part in the plan, slowly spinning in my mind.

It'll take some convincing first, though. I smile, wide, showing my teeth. Whenever I smile with my teeth, I think I look a little deranged, but he seems to enjoy it. "This is the opening I've been waiting for, and you brought it right to me. Thank you so much."

Michail shifts in the armchair, the leather creaking under his fidgeting. I barely spare him a glance. He's no doubt imaging all the ways he can murder Emmanuelle before he leaves my home. Something I can't afford for him to do right now.

Emmanuelle glows under my praise, and I file that little nugget away for analyzing later. "Do you know who else is invited this year?"

"Your friends, Adrian and his Five." He rolls his neck to look at Michail. "I guess four this year if Michail caught indefinite guard duty." He focuses on me again. "You should see if you can get another person to guard you from time to time. I'm sure this one needs regular breaks."

Bickering aside, I close my eyes and focus on the dregs of a plan forming in my mind. It takes seconds since it's not a rather complicated plan. "Thank you again, Emmanuelle, for bringing this invitation."

Michail snorts, and I shoot him a side-eye glare as Emmanuelle takes my hands in his own. "I think this deserves a token of appreciation."

My stomach rolls. The thought of touching this man, even for a second, revolts me. He's sexy. Very sexy in a Harvey Specter sort of way. His clothes are perfect, as is his hair. I just can't bring myself to enjoy him with the same intensity others probably do. Margery would probably like him if she could pin him down long enough to shoot her shot.

I paste on another smile, wait for Michail to turn his face and retreat inside himself wherever he goes to think.

Emmanuelle doesn't like him, though, and is determined to drive a wedge between Michail and me. An all too easy feat with both of us dealing with our own issues currently. "Maybe you can send your little errand boy upstairs to deal with something else? I promise you're safe with me."

It's a naïve sentiment, something I doubt Emmanuelle suffers from. So why is he pushing Michail away and attempting to draw me in? We've barely seen each other over our engagement.

After his last request, he clamps his lips shut and gives me an expectant smile. Oh, he's dead serious.

I glance toward Michail and mime, "Sorry," with my lips. If he sees the word, he doesn't acknowledge it. I resist the urge to reach out and touch his hand as he passes by us on the way to the kitchen.

Emmanuelle faces me again, his legs folded over one another. "Now we can get down to business. I know you're looking for an in to that party. I agree to provide you with anything you need to get you there, but you have to do something for me. Get rid of Adrian's spy for good, and I'll help you in any way I'm able."

I've reached the end of my patience. "You should do that anyway, since we are engaged if you recall."

He catches my hand in his own, my left hand, and shows me my naked ring finger. "It's a little hard to pronounce your engagement when your betrothed doesn't even wear the ring. Did you lose it?"

I jerk my hand from his grasp. "Of course I didn't lose it. I just don't wear it all the time. Only when I need to put on a show. And I can't get rid of Michail. He's one of my brother's men, and my brother doesn't listen to a damn thing I say. Trust me on that one. I could tell Kai the sky is blue, and he'll argue it's green just for the fun of it."

Emmanuelle's smile droops at the corners. "How fascinating. Should I count on you to be at the event? I also need to know if the rumors are true, and there's something going on between you and your bodyguard."

I tense, eyeing the spot where Michail sat earlier. I wish he was still down here. Not that I think Emmanuelle will make a move on me, but because his presence calms and comforts me. It's strange how a short time ago his presence grated on me to no end. Now I just feel warm and safe when I'm with him. "That is none of your business, for one. And two, that is none of your fucking business."

I stand and glare between him and his bodyguards. "You can find your own way out."

Emmanuelle scrambles to regain his composure. He likely has women crawling over each other for his attention. I appreciate a man who can take rejection in stride. It's the only reason I don't hunt down his ring and lob it at his face. That and he and his men got rid of the drive-by shooter.

"We are still engaged, correct?"

I turn as I reach the stairs. "As long as you don't piss me off too much in the meantime, sure."

25

MICHAIL

She creeps down the hallway, checking each room as she passes, looking for me. I shouldn't let her off the hook, but I know what it means to put on an act. She needed to convince Emmanuelle so she can get what she needs from him.

I understand it, but I fucking hate it. Upstairs, I heard what she said to him and what he asked her. Why didn't she end things right there? She told me she would, but maybe that was before...what she said to get me into her bed and nothing more.

I monitor her progress, and the second she breaches the shadows of her bedroom door, I snag her in my arms, one hand over her mouth, the other around her waist, and pull her into the dark.

Her shades are heavy-duty, and there's not much light peeking into the room. But she relaxes, only slightly, enough that her shoulder blades press into my chest, and her heels don't batter against my shins. She knows it's me. That floods me with a sense of awe. This powerful woman recognizes something in me and relaxes at my touch.

No sooner than I relax my grip, she wiggles in my hold, trying to break free again. It's not the same frantic survival kind of fight she's displayed before. No, this is more out of annoyance than anything else. Selena doesn't enjoy being at someone else's mercy. Not if they don't force her to take it.

She breaks free, and I hold up my hands, a smile all for her in place when she rounds on me and shoves at my chest. It's a useless move. I don't shift, but it seems to deflate her enough to keep her from trying to hit me again.

"What the fuck?" she says.

I crowd close, even if she can't see my mirrored anger in her eyes. "You don't get to ask me that when you send me away like the hired fucking help."

Her jaw tightens, and I step toward her bedside table to flip on the lamp. I want to see her eyes when she answers my questions.

"You are the hired fucking help," she hisses. "So I'll treat you any way I see fit."

She says the words, but her voice trails off on the end as if she wishes she could take them back already.

"Please, Princess, tell me what else you think about me. The man who saved your life several times. The man who took your virginity in a screaming orgasm so very recently. You must see something worthy in me to take me to your bed."

She scoffs. "You, more than anyone, know that has nothing to do with fucking someone. I can hate you and fuck you just fine."

Wow. She's delusional, even more than I thought, if she actually believes that to be true. She doesn't hate me anymore than I hate her, but she wants to.

I let the mask slip over my face slowly, giving her time to take it all back, to say something worthy of what is happening between us. I'm not excited about it either, but I'm also not going to run from it the same way she does. When I wear the bored cocky expression I so often adopted as a teenager, her eyes go soft.

"No." I catch her chin hard in my hands and force her head back to look at my face. "No. You don't get to pity me. Not for one damn second. You chose this. Every step of the way, you've made the choice to put distance between us, and you don't get to backtrack the second you get what you want."

She opens her mouth to speak, and I shake my head. I snag the collar of her shirt and rip it, the seams parting easily. With a gasp, she wrenches away, but I don't give up that easily. I tug her back toward me and tear her shirt the rest of the way off. Then her bra, leaving her bare from the waist up.

She doesn't cover herself, only stares at me, jaw rigid, waiting to see what I'll do next.

I go for her pants button and undo them and then jerk her into me to slam my mouth down on hers. She steadies herself by placing a hand on either shoulder, but I'm not allowing her to touch me just yet. Not when she'd so readily cast me aside for someone more like her. I guess that hurts the most if I'm bent on admitting painful truths.

I suck her tongue into my mouth, enjoying the moan she doesn't even know she lets out. A sharp sting on my bottom lip forces me off her. I cut her a glare and touch the pinprick of pain. It's nothing, but a tiny drop of blood comes away from my skin. "You want to play like that?" I whisper.

Her only response is to hike her chin up in challenge. I lean down and drag her bottom lip between my own teeth. I'd never make her bleed, but I bite until she tenses, and then pull away, letting her sensitive flesh slide from between my teeth with the distance. "This isn't about what you want, Princess. For once, you're going to do as you're fucking told and give me what I want."

Her gulp is audible in the silent room. "What do you want?"

I jerk at her pants again, loosening the zipper, and step back to let them hang away from her body. "Take your pants off. Now."

She might have done it for me if I hadn't added the additional command. It's what I expect though. I grasp her around the hips, reverse our positions, and walk her backward toward her very tall bed. When her thighs and my knees hit the frame, "Wha—?" she starts, but I shush her.

"No. Right now, this is for me. This is for how you treated me downstairs in front of your little boyfriend. This is to take the edge off, so we don't kill each other before the job is done. If you agree, do nothing. Hell, fight me if you want. If you don't want me to touch you, then you better speak up now.

I give her a heartbeat, then another. Her anger-filled gaze bores into mine, but she keeps her mouth clamped shut. It's the permission I need. Not that I'm entirely sure I'd have let her walk out of this room anyway.

I peel the tie off my neck and loop it over her head until it's between her teeth, then I tie it off at the back. She shoots me a livid look, fighting harder now.

Not even the tiniest bit gently, I press my hand to her back, forcing her on her belly to the bed. To my surprise, she stays, and I don't get a headbutt for the effort when I bend down and strip her pants and underwear off her at her ankles.

Standing again, I press my hand to the center of her back. She looks so fragile in my hold, her muscles tensing hard as I explore the softness of her skin here.

"What the fuck are you doing?" she asks through the gag.

I fold my body over her so she can feel my cock against her ass through my pants. Her eyes go wide, and she drops her forehead onto the bed, her back rising and falling harder under my hand.

I kick off my own pants and underwear in seconds and enjoy the way my cock looks planted between the round globes of her ass. It's almost obscene in the best fucking way possible. "Do you know how beautiful you are like this? So much power, and for right now, you belong to me."

She doesn't answer me, and I don't expect her to. This is more of a punishment than making love. I want her to learn she belongs to me in every way, and if I have to rub my cum into her skin at every opportunity to accomplish that, then so be it.

I reach down and nudge her thighs wider, testing the entrance of her pussy for the slickness I already know is there. She's molten fire against my hand, and so wet she's practically dripping. "That's it, Princess. You're going to take me so well right now. I can feel it."

I line my cock up with her entrance and slowly, so very slowly, ease inside her body. She wiggles and tenses as I progress, soft heady moans escaping every so often.

When my front is flush with her hips, I rearrange her legs but end up grabbing her hips, lifting her slightly so she dances barely on her tiptoes. The angle feels perfect, and I revel in the push and pull as I slide from her body, almost completely out of her tight little cunt, and then back in.

She curses and mumbles against the gag, but I ignore her mouth, too focused on the way she squeezes me with each stroke. How she presses back into me each time I try to retreat. She wants me so much more than she can admit to herself. Something in me is determined to make her see it.

I drop her feet flat to the floor and squat enough to get the angle back the way I want it. Then I snake my hand to her front and brush my thumb over her clit. Her body tenses like she got struck by lightning, and I feel it around my cock too. "Yes," I encourage her. "You want it so bad, baby. I'm going to make you come before I take mine."

I increase my pace, adding another finger, rubbing her harder. She pushes back against me still, as if she's trying to fuck me from the front, but I keep things controlled, too slow for her wants, but fast enough that she's panting for more.

"This is how I always want you, Princess. Bound, gagged, spread open for me and me alone. I want to feast on you every way possible, and when you think you can't possibly take anymore, I'll fuck that sweet little asshole too. I'll make every inch of you mine. You won't even realize it's done until it's too late."

She moans, and I fuck into her harder, enjoying the sounds of our bodies slapping together in a carnal rhythm as old as time itself. Humans may have added shame to sex, but there's nothing shameful about this. Nothing unworthy about the trust she's given me, even as she professes loathing for every part of me.

My orgasm builds white hot in seconds, but I refuse to allow myself release until I feel her milk it out of me. "Come for me, baby. Take it all."

She explodes with a gasp, followed by a moan, and her body relaxes on the mattress as she rides the sensation out. I keep hold of her hip, move my hand from her clit, and grasp her other side.

It's my turn.

I pound into her at a brutal pace, slamming us together. Then, right as I'm about to blow my load, I slide as deep as possible and insert my thumb into her tight little ring of muscles spread open for my gaze right now.

Her entire body goes taut like a bowstring, and she comes again, milking my end so beautifully, I see stars. I pull out, even as everything in my brain is screaming at me not to, and pump my cum onto her muscular back. It streaks across her skin in bursts until I'm done and wipe the head of my cock on her ass cheek.

My knees wobble in the aftermath, and I have to take a few steadying breaths before I can free myself. I reach up and untie the gag. Now free, she crawls up on the bed.

"Stop," I order, and head into the bathroom for a towel.

I wash her skin gently, even between her legs, and let her roll over on her back. She stares up at me, something soft in her eyes. "I hate you," she whispers.

I stare down at her. No doubt my mask has slipped away without me even realizing it. She's looking at the core of me. "I hate you too," and I mean the exact opposite.

26

SELENA

In the still, dark hours of early morning, I peel myself out of bed. The sheets are cold. Michail is gone, and I rub my chest where the realization hurts. It doesn't matter. He hates me as much as I wish I hated him. I'll keep shoving him away for his own good.

I stretch, enjoying the tight tender sensations rolling through my well-used body. A hot shower helps loosen things more, and I stare at my dopey smile in the mirror for a heartbeat. Then let it slip away. No. I have too much at stake to risk it all for what? Good sex.

It's a lie, and I know it. But I'm good at convincing myself that lies are true.

Though the upstairs is full of shadows, I don't bother flipping the lights as I descend into the soft glow emanating from the kitchen. Michail is standing at the stove, clad only in his underwear, cooking something.

The scent of garlic and peppers reaches me before the soft pop and sizzle of the food in the pan. I quietly enter the kitchen and skirt around the edge to take one of the stools opposite where he's cooking. He meets my eyes for only a second and then focuses back on his work. Sausage, onions, and an array of vegetables sizzle in the pan, creating an aroma which sets my stomach growling violently. I realize I hadn't eaten the day before. Not with all the excitement.

"Did you get any sleep?" I venture, latching on to a subject that will hopefully allow us a conversation without a fight.

"Only a couple of hours. Your brother has been calling us both repeatedly. I haven't answered him back yet. If he asks, I'll admit to the attempt on your life yesterday, and he'll back off some."

I wave him away and dig the phone out of the pocket of my lavender silk pajama pants. It takes seconds to find my brother's text string and shoot him a message. He might want to treat me like a child at every turn, but he needs to remember that I can take care of myself. I have been doing so for years. With Julia off killing people in various, creative ways, and Kai hacking his way, both literally and figuratively, through Adrian's enemies, I've been left to my own devices.

The second I took my seat on the council, my parents jetted off to Florida, or anywhere the sun can turn their pale skin to a warm glow. I don't envy their freedom. They served our community well for years, but they were my lifeline for so long, I didn't realize how alone I've felt until Michail came into my life. And now I have to keep him out of all of this. He's made it clear what he thinks of my world. He'll never stand stoically at my side to create the partnership my parents cultivated.

It's not in the cards for us, and I'm coming to accept it. For right now, I can have him. For as long as he can stand to be near me and touch me, I'll keep him.

"What's that look on your face for?"

His voice breaks my thoughts, and I drag my eyes from the screen of my phone to his tense face. He's pulled his curls back, not in a ponytail but with a thin black headband, just enough to keep it out of his way. With his hair this way, he looks younger, and far more handsomely devastating.

I curb the lust which fires through me and place my phone on the counter softly. "It's nothing. I was just thinking about my parents. I guess I miss them a little bit."

He shuffles the food around the pan, sending another scent cloud between us. "It's okay to feel things, you know? To love, to hate, to feel longing..." He trails off, and I wait to see if he's going to elaborate.

When he doesn't, I plant my chin on my hands and regard him sadly. "It might be okay for normal people, but not for me. Not councilmembers, not some of the society who keeps things running smoothly. You as well as anyone know how keenly emotion can be honed into a weapon. And those kinds of weapons hurt more than any other."

"Is that why you've pushed your brother away all these years? Why you ignore your sister's text messages?"

I glance at my phone, my mouth hanging open. "How did you... stay the fuck out of my phone. It's none of your business."

He cuts the heat on the burner and pours the stir-fry between two plates. "As I told you before, everything about you is my business, especially when I'm charged to protect you."

This time, his dictate sounds softer, less like an obligation and more like a plea.

I nod and accept the plate he hands me. He ambles around to my side of the counter and takes the stool next to mine. Our elbows graze, and I ignore the sharp shoot of longing which rolls through me at the simple touch.

Fucking hell. I'm in so much trouble. I blow on a bite of the food and then take a tentative nibble. Flavor bursts in my mouth, and I shove a whole steaming heap into my face and chew fast. When I swallow, I find him staring at me, chewing slowly, methodically. There's heat in his eyes and the tiniest hint of humor at the corner of his upturned lips.

I point at the plate with my fork. "This is so good. I feel like I haven't eaten anything in forever."

"You haven't," he notes, turning his attention back to his own plate. "Are you going to tell me about this event we're going to crash?"

I nod, finish chewing, and shift on the stool to face him. "It's an annual charity event. Everyone will be there. Once we are in, we can easily overtake any resistance and get my seat back. I'll have allies there, friends, and with me in front of them demanding the allegiance, they promised they won't be able to refuse me."

His shoulders tighten, and I let myself look my fill before going back to my meal. It takes so long for him to speak I'm wondering if I said something to upset him.

"I don't think you understand how volatile this situation may be." His tone is soft, as if he fears my reaction.

Only because of his halting tone do I think about what he's saying. Usually, he says something, I say something back that contradicts what he's saying, all of it more of a fight than a conversation. Nothing more than bids for dominance in a world where I don't actually want to be top dog. Yes, I want my council seat. I want to watch over my people. But in Michail's arms, I want him to take control. Something tells me he likes to fight me for it every time.

After swallowing a lump in my throat, I take a sip of water to give myself more time. "I understand what you are saying. I'd like to go anyway, and if things look dicey, we can leave. The event space will be packed, and it's a masquerade. No one will notice me until I choose to be noticed."

He eats a few more bites of food and nods into his plate. "Fine, we'll go if that's what you want, but you'll be armed in as many ways as we can manage before we head in there."

I smile, knowing how much it means when he gives in to something he's dead set against. He's more hardheaded and stubborn than I am.

We finish our food, and I wash the dishes quickly. I usually never cook at home, so this was a rare treat.

When I'm done, I find him in my office, staring down at his laptop from the armchair in the corner. He points to a huge box in the center of the room. "Your fiancé sent you a present." His tone is biting, and I hide my flinch as I circle the box.

"Are you sure it's from him?"

He nods, eyes on his screen. "He brought it personally."

I gently pry the white lid from the top of the box and part the creamy tissue paper. Nestled inside is an array of dresses all in various colors, cuts, but every single one in my size.

"He sent you fucking clothes?" Michail asks, craning his neck for a look over the edge of the box. "Doesn't he know how much you hate when men try to dress you up like a barbie doll? You aren't wearing one of those with me on your arm."

I pull out the first dress, a champagne number with soft tulle skirts. It's feminine and in no way my style. I lay it gently aside. "There's a difference. He sent me multiple things to choose from, and while I don't generally like clothing as a gift, these are lovely. Also, you won't be by my side. I have to go with Emmanuelle. It will be expected."

A sharp crack splits the room, and I jerk my head up. He's thrown something from his spot to the far wall. "What happened to no one will recognize you? If you're with Emmanuelle, everyone will recognize you."

I shrug, cataloging each dress. All of them are lovely, but none my taste. "Maybe in your city. Here, with both of us in masks, no one will suspect a thing. There's no way anyone can recognize him that way."

"You are naïve if you think this is all going to go according to your half-assed plans."

I shove off the box, using it for leverage to gain my footing. "And you're jealous, which is why you're being such a dick right now."

We lasted a whole hour without fighting, a new record for us. "I'm going back to bed, and you can stay down here or in the guest room for all I care."

Michail picks up his phone, his eyes locked with mine, and

quickly taps out what I assume is a text. Then he places it back beside his laptop and throws me a challenging look.

My phone vibrates, and I'm about to call him childish for texting me when I'm standing two feet in front of him, but the text isn't from him. It's from Kai.

I don't even bother opening it before glaring. "Are you fucking kidding me? You tattled to my brother because I'm not doing things your way? Very mature."

I stalk out of the room, and my brother calls this time. Apparently, I didn't answer his text fast enough at three in the morning. I hit the accept button, hold the phone to my ear, and bark out a "What?"

"What the hell are you thinking? You can't go into this thing with a stranger on your arm and no backup. Not to mention we need to talk about your little race off into the night first. What the fuck is wrong with you? I'm trying to keep you safe."

"By locking me up? How is that going to help me get my council seat back? Newsflash, it won't. If I don't have this, I have nothing. Goodnight brother, don't call me again unless you have something useful to offer."

I hit the end button and turn to Michail standing in the doorway. With his hip cocked against the frame and his arms crossed over his chest, I can tell he's unamused. Good. So am I.

I glare all the way up the stairs until he is out of sight. Why do all these men think they can control my every move? I'm done fucking allowing it.

27

MICHAIL

I pack my bag in the dark. It's a cowardly move, but what does she expect? She won't let me keep her safe, and with her fiancé's men roaming outside, she doesn't really need me anyway. At least it's the lie, I tell myself.

One of the guards, a man with arms twice as big as Kai's, steps aside to allow me out of the townhouse. His eyes stay locked on my back, and I have little doubt that all of Emmanuelle's guards know exactly what services I've been providing Selena, if their glares and curled lips are any sign.

I throw my bag in the back of my car, climb behind the wheel, and sit. Simply sit. I don't start the vehicle; I don't check my phone. I stay in stillness.

Sometimes, it keeps me from going off the deep end, but right now, I want to fling myself over the edge. Consequences be damned. What if I walk back into the house, pack a bag for her, and we leave? Run away where none of this bullshit can find us?

It's a pretty fantasy, but not one she'll indulge. Not after fighting so hard to keep her little piece of power. The sad part is she thinks her seat as the lead councilwoman defines who she is. But I've witnessed her strength, her weakness, her kindness, and the tiny kernel of hope she fears showing anyone else. It's barely budding, but she keeps it alive all the same.

My phone vibrates in my pocket, and I tease it out and glance at the screen. I don't recognize the number, and it's late for social calls. If I had even a little bit of a social life to begin with. Curious, more than anything, I hit the accept button and press the phone to my ear.

"Hello?"

"Mich? Is that you?" Her voice ices my blood. I don't need to ask who it is.

I let out a long-controlled breath, slipping into one of my many guises, letting it infiltrate me, chase away that ice and replace it with something she'll recognize, connect with. "Margery, you called. I didn't think you had my number."

"I'm very good at finding things when I have interest," she says, soft and throaty like she's imparting a secret.

For a second, my act falters, splinters, and blinding rage forces its way through me like a very sharp knife to a very vulnerable gut. I shake it away, closing my eyes to sell the story to even myself. "I don't doubt that for a second. You're a powerful woman. You can have whatever you want."

I can hear the smile in her tone as she answers. "Oh, you charmer. Well, to be honest, I'm calling to see if you'd like to be my escort to an event tomorrow night. I know it's last minute, but I'm happy to send you the proper attire. It is for charity as well."

I pop open my eyes, something flinty sharpening inside me. This is exactly the opening I need. It allows me to go to the event and not have to worry about what kind of story I'll need to make up to find my way inside. Selena won't be as alone as she expects.

It takes little effort to force brightness into my response. "I'd be delighted to attend with you, Margery." I draw out her name, making her feel it. "Should I meet you at the event space, or would you prefer me to pick you up?"

"Oh, don't trouble yourself. Meet me there. I'll send an invite around to Selena's home, shall I? I think she mentioned you were staying with her."

It's a question and a trap. One I'm not stupid enough to fall into. "Of course. Yes, I'm here for now, until her brother recalls me to another task."

She makes an agreeing noise. "See you at eight o'clock."

"I'm looking forward to it."

She clicks off, and I lower the phone to my lap and sling my head back into the car seat. Looks like I don't get to leave quite yet. This is a gift. I've dreamed about the day I would sink my blade into this woman's heart for years. Ever since the day she paid to "rent" my body and then throw me out like trash. It's not the discarding that stuck with me, it's the depraved things she wanted to do with my then much scrawnier sixteen-year-old body. She's sick, twisted, and the perfect customer for the likes of Sal's fucking family.

I grab my bag and go back into the house. It's quiet, the lights are off, and I settle back into the guest room even as I imagine curling up behind Selena. I can't though, not when I need to get into the headspace for what I'm about to do.

After breakfast the next day, I find Selena in the study. Another large clothing box sits in the center. "You decide you need a different dress for tonight?"

She looks up from her computer, her eyes focusing as if I pulled her attention from far away. "Oh, no. That's for you. Apparently, you made quite the impression on my friend Margery." There's a hint of jealousy in her tone, but I don't have time to savor it since I'm focused on her words.

Her friend Margery.

I barely keep my lip from curling. Margery's only friends are ambition and treachery. She might have loved her husband once. Maybe enough to spare him some pain when he, so tragically—and conveniently—died years ago.

I kneel on the floor and lift the lid off the box. Inside is a tuxedo, and it disturbs me she thinks she has my measure so easily.

This is a challenge, and a claim of ownership all at once.

Selena comes around her desk to peer into the box. "Oh, she sent you a tuxedo?"

I slide the lid in place again and stand. "She asked me to be her date for the charity event tonight."

Barely a flicker shows on her face at my news, and it's a punch in the gut. Only a few short nights ago she laid claim to me, just as I did her long before then. Now, she's just going to ignore the fact that another woman is trying to cut in. Friend or not? The only reason I haven't gutted Emmanuelle already is because Adrian forbade it immediately after Andrea's attack. He didn't explain himself, but he rarely does until he finds it necessary, at least to anyone who isn't Kai.

Selena stoops and pulls the suit from the box. "You should go hang it up so the wrinkles will fall out. There's a steamer in the bathroom, or I can call someone to take care of it."

I take the suit from her carefully. "I've got it. Sorry to interrupt whatever you are doing."

She shakes her head and sits behind her desk again. "Don't worry about it. I was reviewing some society connections, hoping to figure out who is intent on taking me out. If I can identify them, then I can know how they got others on their side. It'll mean for an easier shift back to how things are supposed to be."

Lost in thought, she's completely forgotten about me, and I slip out of the room to take the suit upstairs. The idea of wearing it disgusts me, but donning the clothes she provided, acknowledging the ownership in the fact, will give me an advantage.

I lay the suit on my bed, but before I can go find the steamer Selena mentioned, my phone ringing cuts through the silence. I answer immediately, knowing the distinct ringer I set for Adrian.

"Boss?"

His voice is frosted over. Ice with zero give. "Where the fuck are you right now?"

I have nothing to fear from Adrian, so I tell him the truth. "At Selena's townhouse. I kept tabs on her when she snuck out the other night. I've been staying in her guest room."

"And this party tonight?"

I'm not sure what he wants me to say. "I'll be there. Attending with another society member here. Selena will be escorted by her fiancé."

Adrian makes a rough noise low in his throat. "What's going on, Mich? It's not like you to run off without a word and sit on an unsanctioned job."

I slide onto my bed and sigh. "It's nothing. I just need to make sure she's safe before I can come back home."

"It's like that, huh?" His voice is deadly soft.

I don't acknowledge or deny the implication in his voice. "I'll be home once this is done, and Selena is back where she belongs."

Adrian chuckles softly. It's a sound that usually strikes fear into people. Anyone who isn't family. "Good luck with that."

He doesn't say goodbye, and I wonder why he's calling now. I've been away for weeks, and he calls now?

I glance down at the suit. Knowing the brand, it costs as much as some of the ones Kai owns. The thought of putting it on makes nausea rise in my gut.

"You okay?" Selena asks from my open doorway.

I stare down at my phone, still in my hands. "Fine. I'm fine."

She crosses the room, stopping in front of me to lift my chin. I meet her eyes, and I can't handle what she doesn't think to hide this time. Not while she wears another man's ring. Not while she's trying to do everything she can to ensure we'll never be together. Not while I want nothing more than to pull her into my arms and bury myself in the feel of her. "You can talk to me. I'm a shitty listener, but a very good shot with a gun."

I snort. "I'm fine, really. Just tired. It's been a few long nights, remember?"

Her eyes go dreamy, and she gives me a curt nod, stepping away. "Right. Well. You can ride with us to the event if you want."

I want to keep the peace a little longer, so I don't detail how much I absolutely don't want to be trapped in a limo with her and the man she's pretending she'll marry. "I'll take my car."

She backs toward the door, giving me one last look. "Well, okay then. I'll see you there. I bet you're going to look great in that. Don't let her drink too much though. She gets handsy when she's drunk. You have no idea how many young waiters she's had to pay off to keep them quiet."

Before she disappears, I call her back. She pokes her head into the room again. I don't know what makes me ask her, maybe the stupid budding, barely standing, hope I have in my body. "If you weren't meant to rule this seat of power, what do you think you'd do?"

Her forehead crumples as she considers. "I don't know. Maybe something with numbers. I'm very good at making money. It's one reason I rose to my position at such a young age. There is nothing the society loves more than money."

I nod, and she smiles, a flash of a thing, there and gone. Along with her.

She's right. There's nothing that moves mountains amongst criminals like money. So who in this Chicago set has the most cash to throw around?

It's a question I'd like answered before I walk into the middle of this mess. That party could very well be a trap, and I'd rather die than allow her to be hurt again. So finding out who's got my little brat in their sights is my first priority. Margery might very well help me there if I play my cards right. Do something useful with her disgusting life before I end it.

The state of the money in her little patch of land isn't something

I'm going to ask Selena about, but I shoot Kai a text asking him to look into it.

I stand and face the tuxedo. She wants to wrap me up like a present so she can peel off the layers later.

I swallow hard, leaning forward in case the bile stinging my throat actually comes up. This is going to take one hell of an act to get through, but the reward will be worth it. I can't wait to see the look on Margery's face when I cut out her heart inch by painful inch.

28

SELENA

Usually, I enjoy preparing for a party. Now, after everything that's happened and the weeks I've been away, I'm not sure how to face it. How to face these people who were so quick to see me betrayed.

I decide to wear one of the dresses Emmanuelle sent, since the obscenely feminine cut and sparkling tulle will provide the perfect disguise. There will be some there who will recognize me. I can only hope my presence stays a secret long enough for me to make a move.

I finish my makeup and leave my hair loose and curly. I already hate the sewn in beads of the bodice and how they dig into my skin. I'll be peppered in little red dots later. At least the champagne color is pretty, and I have shoes to match already.

Emmanuelle arrives five minutes before he said he would. All in all, he's not a bad guy. In my research, I didn't discover much about his activity on his council, or anything about his family or holdings. Usually people without family connections don't make it on the council. It's too easy to usurp those who have no backup when the shit hits the fan.

I slide the engagement ring on my finger and slip my phone into my clutch. Emmanuelle holds out a mask, which I allow him to tie around the back of my hair. When I face him again, he gives me a cursory glance, but there's no heat. None of the fire Michail usually pins me with.

As usual, he's immaculate. His hair is styled in a soft wave, his five o'clock shadow trimmed and rugged. Even the midnight blue of his velvet tuxedo brings out the gold flecks in his eyes.

"Ready?" There's a little grin on his lips as if he knows I was checking him out.

"Yes. Let's get this over with."

He leads me to his car, and I clip my seatbelt while he climbs into the backseat beside me. As we wind through traffic, I shift to face him, the scratchy material of my dress screeching over the leather underneath us. "I would like to go over the plan one more time."

He shrugs as if he doesn't care one way or the other, his attention out the window and not on me. Taking him at his word and hoping he's paying attention, I try to make sense of the thing in my brain. "We'll go inside and get the lay of things. The council doesn't usually meet until at least mid-way through any event. They hear petitions, etcetera, before the ending remarks."

Emmanuelle flicks his eyes to my face. "I'm well aware of the protocol, holding a seat myself."

I rush on. "I figure that will be the perfect time to strike. We'll see who is sitting in my seat, and then I can take it from there. No one in that room is completely invulnerable, and I know everyone's weakness."

"Everyone's?"

At first, I think he's mocking me, but his face is deadly serious.

"Everyone on the council," I elaborate.

He only narrows his eyes, studying me. "And do they know your weakness? Oh, wait, they wouldn't since you've only just developed it recently." There is a hint of mockery now, and more than a little edge.

"Excuse me?" Since the day we met, outside of our negotiations, he's been nothing but kind, steadfast even. What's changed now?

I scan his features. There's no way he could have fallen in love with me, and I know damn well he never expected me to follow through with this marriage. He would have been happy to take me to his bed, but neither of us were planning to walk down that aisle.

When he doesn't respond, I press. I need this to go off without a hitch. Otherwise, people will die, and I can't have more dead bodies on my conscience. "Are you all right?"

He leans forward and braces his elbows on his knees to cradle his face. "My apologies. I'm just having a rough day. I almost canceled on you tonight, but I know what this means for you, and I didn't want to let you down the one time you actually asked for my help."

"What is this whole thing really about? Shoring up connections, fine, I get that, but why me? Especially when I've lost my seat?"

He rubs his hands over his head and somehow it doesn't mess up his perfectly-styled hair one bit. "You're going to think I'm a fucking lunatic."

Now I'm just intrigued. I can't help the smile spreading across my lips. "Now you have to tell me. What is it? A bet? Blackmail?"

"A woman."

That's not the answer I expect, considering I'm wearing his engagement ring. But things slide into place when I consider it. No wonder he agreed to my demands so easily. It was a sham on his part too. "Who? Anyone I know?"

It hits me from the tortured look on his face. "Andrea? Are you talking about Andrea? She seemed into you the other night. But I doubt taking her to propose to someone else is going to endear her to you."

He settles into the seat again, turning his eyes out the window to the passing buildings. "I got caught in something stupid a while back. It's made it impossible for me to...for us to..."

Now I'm really confused, but he goes silent, not elaborating any further. I lean into the seat, my dress scratching me and the leather further. How did he think proposing to me would win him her attention? Unless there's something at play I haven't realized yet.

There's no time to question him further. We pull up outside the event space, and Emmanuelle helps me out of the car. A cadre of his oversized bodyguards follow us inside.

As usual, everything is stunning. Our society goes all out for charity events, and this year is no exception. The place is packed, and I spot more than a few faces I recognize. It's kind of fun being here in disguise. If only my stomach didn't take up residence in my throat since the moment we crossed the threshold.

Emmanuelle takes my arm, and I wish, for a second, he was Michail. That I walked in with the man I actually want on my arm.

We slip through the crowd, his guards fanning out behind us. I keep my eyes out for people I know, ones I trust to have my back, but there are decidedly few here. Until I hear a soft masculine laugh. I jerk my face toward him, spotting him even with a hundred people around us.

Margery is clutching him to her side, her thin body hugged tight in a dress belonging on a sixteen-year-old girl heading to prom. What is she thinking?

Then Michail turns, and I can't stop looking at him. Damn, I give her props for her ability to dress a man. His suit is just the tiniest bit too tight, and I don't mind one single bit. All of him is on display, and the appreciation I feel quickly shifts to something sharper.

As does the gut kick I get when he flashes her a sexy grin. I recognize the look on his face as one of the masks he slips into. I think he calls this one beautiful and stupid. A role he plays more often than I wish he would.

Emmanuelle slides a champagne glass into my hand. I give him an appreciative smile. "Thank you."

His eyes trail to Michail and then to me. His phone dings loudly in his pocket and he tugs it out to check, his eyes wary. Then he smooths his features and focuses on the scene once more.

Part of me wants to ask what that's about, but we aren't friends enough, and whatever he's dealing with is none of my business.

He skirts around me, heading toward them, and I have to stumble to keep up. Emmanuelle takes Margery's hand, kisses it, tucks it onto his arm. "Forgive me, but I want to dance with the most beautiful woman in the room."

She twitters, and I step out of the way to allow them access to the dance floor. I turn to face Michail again, and he's staring narrow-eyed at Emmanuelle's back. Then he drops his gaze to me, and it's like I can let my shoulders fall away from my ears for the first time all day.

"Dance?" He extends his arm for me to take.

I nod and let him lead me to the floor. I'm not sure what to expect with him, but he leads me through a waltz expertly. So perfectly, in fact, for once I don't have to consider the steps. "Are you ready?" he asks.

It takes me a second to realize he's not talking about dancing. I shake myself to focus. Which seems impossible with the lemongrass scent of him surrounding me. With the heat of him pressing in.

A clock chimes somewhere, and I know it's the call for the councilmembers to meet in the chambers. Bitterness coats my tongue. Chambers that I have to force my way into now.

Michail tips my chin up and brushes his thumb over my lip. Then he's gone.

Emmanuelle joins me and leads me to the bar. The crowd has thinned with the council's exit and a lot of attendees have adjourned to eat until they return. Especially if they don't have business with them.

Minutes tick by, and I have to keep myself from fidgeting. I sip some water that I snag off a passing waiter and scan the crowd for Emmanuelle's men. Do they know what kind of man they serve? Or are they his friends like the five serve Adrian? We've been fake engaged for a while now, and I barely know anything about him.

While I don't have any romantic notions, I wouldn't mind being his friend. Which gives me pause since I haven't allowed myself to want friendship from anyone in a very long time. I guess seeing how devoted Adrian's Five are to him, and how they also serve my brother, not only serve but love him, I crave those kinds of connections too. Hell, my entire world fell apart, and I didn't have anyone to turn to except my brother. And even then, I felt like he helped me more out of familiar obligation than actual desire. I haven't exactly been an angel, nor gone out of my way to help him in the past. The brush with his councilwoman was my first attempt at making things right between us, and even then, he still only saw me as the power-hungry sister who would step on her family to reach her goals.

Emmanuelle leads me through the crowd toward the council chamber doors. Huge columns bracket the giant double doors, adding an air of majesty I always loved about this place.

I brace my shoulders, readying myself and my mask for what I might find on the other side of that door. It's time to finally face the person responsible for the attacks, and all the pain I've had to deal with in recent weeks.

A tiny, bloodthirsty part of me wants to see their head on a pike in my front yard. My neighbors likely won't appreciate my yard ornaments like I do. Michail would though. Hell, he'd string up tiki lights just to draw more attention to it.

Emmanuelle gives my hand one last squeeze as his men rush forward and charge the chamber doors. They open inward, startling those around us into silence.

I reach behind me, untie the mask, and let it fall away. But I don't get the satisfying revelation I am expecting.

The chamber is the same as it ever was. Each chair set off the floor like a throne. Several men sit, bored expressions on their faces, but when I get to the center chair, my heart threatens to crawl out of my mouth.

Margery is sitting there, back perfectly straight, one hand on the arm of the chair, the other entwined in Michail's curls. He's kneeling at her feet, slightly drooping to the side. His hands are tied behind his back, and his face is pressed against her knee like a dog.

What the fuck is happening here? I have to stare, my brain skipping the details as if it's trying to protect me.

The world tilts under my feet. Not at my friend's betrayal. I learned a long time ago not to trust anyone. But since I've been stuck with Michail, he's shown me there are some people I can trust.

And right now, this bitch has him tied at her feet like a dog. A white-hot flash of heat, of anger, makes my ears burn, and I clench my fists so no one can see them tremble. I'm not fucking scared, and I don't want anyone to assume I am, because I'm about to cut this bitch and make her watch me measure her fucking entrails.

Margery waves her hand regally. "Please, join us. We have much to discuss."

29

MICHAIL

The very distinct metallic snick of multiple guns being cocked in tandem catches my attention. Except, I'm not even sure where I am or what's happening. I remember dancing with Selena, and then everything goes hazy.

I sit up straight, a headache pounding between my eyes. At the same time, I register several things. Margery has her fingers in my hair, digging the sharp points into my scalp. There are men surrounding the room, all armed, all pointing weapons at the little crowd just inside the doorway.

Selena.

She's staring at me, her eyes hooded, her beautiful jaw set. I try to keep my eyes open so I can see her, blinking to clear some of the haze in my mind.

The bitch drugged me. It must have been in the champagne she offered me as we exited toward the council chambers. My knees ache faintly, and the cold marble under me isn't doing me any favors.

I cut my gaze to Selena again who is talking to Margery, I presume, but I can't catch the words, each one slipping away as I try to focus.

The only reason I'm awake for this is because Margery underestimated how much drug she should have slipped me. Small mercies.

I try to work the knots at my wrist, the thin rope easy to manipulate for someone with a lot of practice with being tied up. Not to mention she favored the same knots as she did when I was a teenager. Convenient.

There's some loud shouting, and I resettle my shoulders, still feigning the drug is hitting me harder than it actually is.

Margery caresses my scalp and whispers an endearment in a baby voice like one might address a dog.

I can't wait to stab this bitch. My fingers are itching for it. I want to see the light leave her eyes and revel in the satisfaction that I took one more asshole off the streets.

I have to play this perfectly. The drugs are already in my system, and I know my reflexes are slower than usual. I can't risk attacking one of these goons. It's likely they'll shoot me before I can take a weapon.

But it's not the guards I need to fool. It's the psychopath on the throne.

I continue loosening the knots and let out a low moan, leaning farther against her. She gives me another proprietary pat, her attention fully focused on Selena.

Selena's voice filters into the haze, slowly, like a overlaid audio file just barely off track with a movie scene. "What's going on here?"

I keep my eye on Selena, through the fall of my curls. That tone. She's pissed as fuck and about to rain hell down on everyone here. I keep hiding and watching.

Waiting to see her in her pissed off glory.

She takes a few steps forward, Emmanuelle joining her despite the wary eye he keeps on all the guns in the room.

The numerous guards wear the typical uniform here: black cargos, black turtleneck, black ski mask. Not sure who thought that was a good idea, especially in summer, but who am I to complain? A couple of them accent their uniform with a small pin, but I can't make out the symbol in the drug haze. Not that it matters anyway.

I finish loosening the knots but keep my movement lethargic as I separate my hands.

Selena is closer now than when I last looked up. I try to glare, get her attention somewhere, but she's refusing to look at me. As if I'm beneath her.

It's an act. If she pretends I mean nothing, Margery loses her bargaining chip. A good tactic if Margery has every intention of keeping me alive so I can become her bed slave or something equally disgusting.

So, I stop trying to get her attention and focus on Emmanuelle. He stares around the room, glaring at the guards. Hell, he looks downright mutinous, as if their presence has foiled all his carefully laid plans. I suppose they have, but Margery is the ringleader. If anyone deserves his ire, it's her.

Selena is closer now, so close I can smell her perfume. I slowly breathe her in, allowing the scent of her to chase a little more of the fog away.

No, if Selena is near enough, Margery will downright kill her. The only reason she's not lying on the floor in a pool of her own blood is because Margery likes the show, the attention, and the intrigue to go along with it. Like villains on TV, she wants to monologue about her rise to power and all that.

It's enough to make me want to kill her all over again.

Everything in me is screaming out to Selena. I wish she'd run. Get out of her and leave me. Margery isn't going to kill me anytime soon. She can regroup, call her brother, do so many things that aren't standing here arguing with a crazy person.

Selena stands her ground though. "I want you out of my seat and out of my city. In exchange, I won't kill you."

Of course, Margery laughs. "You don't have the power to kill me. I'm not sure if you noticed the several rifles trained on you right now? Besides, wouldn't you rather bargain for your little pet here?"

Selena shrugs, seemingly unconcerned, but I can see the clench of her fists. She's pissed as hell and ready for a fight. "He means nothing to me. As you said, he's beautiful. A pet and nothing more."

The words cut deep even as I tell myself she doesn't mean it. She's only telling Margery what she wants to hear, what she expects to hear.

I moan again for effect, drawing Margery's attention. She leans down and pats my cheek. "Oh, no. I think I gave you too much. You won't be able to perform your duties for me later."

A wave of nausea gut punches me hard, and this time I don't have to fake a noise.

"Don't worry," she tells me, not meeting my eyes but looking at me like an object. "We'll make sure you're good to go when the time is right."

Sickness roils in my gut, and I look around to see who's a witness, who's a party to this bitch's actions. The councilmembers around the room monitor the situation from their perspective thrones, yet they stay quiet. They do nothing.

From their pallor and the way they all watch the door like it can save them, more than a few of them are disturbed by Margery's display of me for her own amusement. Maybe I'll kill them quickly instead of making them suffer.

Maybe.

Selena sighs loudly, as if she's bored, but I can still hear the fine thread of fury underneath. "I told you to leave, and I'll give you five more minutes to make it happen."

Another cock of a gun reaches me, but I'm not fast enough. Margery is up with the barrel pressed into Selena's forehead before I can pry my languid limbs off the marble.

"Or," Margery says conversationally, "we can try this another way.

You say goodbye to your pet, walk out of here, leave my city, and I'll allow you to live."

I shove my hair out of my face to keep a better eye on them. The guards around the room have moved closer, closing ranks inside the ring of chairs instead of outside. Emmanuelle and his men hover near the door, waiting to see what happens. Hopefully, looking for an opening.

Well, I'm not waiting for that shit. It takes me what feels like a full minute to get upright. I keep my hands behind my back as if I'm still tied, and stumble toward the two women.

I lean into Margery, my head on her shoulder. She smiles at Selena. "See, he wants me, not you. So, take the deal."

I lift my head and pin her with a look. One I hope she can read through the mask I'm wearing. "It's easy, Selena. You simply kiss my cheek, tell me you had fun, and walk away."

She drags her eyes to mine, and the room seems to shrink around us. "What?" she says, her voice trembling for the first time since she walked in.

I step forward, between Selena and the gun Margery is holding, and stare down into her eyes. "Kiss my cheek. Tell me you had fun. Walk away."

My words are strained, and I hope Margery thinks it's from the drugs. What she can't see are the hot tears swimming in my eyes, or how hard I'm grinding my teeth together to keep my mask in place.

Selena sobs once, a tear trailing down her cheek. I swipe it away and lean down so she can do as I've directed. She dutifully brushes her lips across my cheek.

Upright again, I nod tightly, just once. "Tell me you had fun."

She presses her mouth together.

Margery huffs from behind me. "Move, just let me shoot her, and we can all get on with our damn night."

I don't budge, keeping my eyes locked on Selena. An entire world passes between us. Everything I've ever wanted to say, and everything she's kept from me. After what feels like a lifetime, she whispers, "I had fun."

Each syllable slices me open. My knees wobble as my body fights the drugs and tries to keep me upright at the same time.

I swallow the lump in my throat, tears still swimming in my eyes, threatening to fall any second. "Now walk away," I prompt.

She stares at me longer, the tears pouring down her cheeks now. I catch a whisper of, "I can't."

Equally as soft, I say, "You can, because you have to. You are the one who needs to live."

Then I raise my voice, sharpening my tone. "Walk the fuck away."

She jolts at my shout, and Margery snickers from behind me.

Selena's shoulders settle back, her chin inching higher, and I know I've won. It's a hollow victory. No one is a winner here. It's just one broken heart after one broken heart, and people too dumb to admit the truth to each other.

She takes one step backward, one single step, and it's as if my entire world's been ripped in two. Of course, I want her to go, to be safe, away from all of this. But watching her leave is one heartbreak too many over a lifetime of nothing but trauma and fear.

The only thing that kept me going all these years was Adrian. The Five. My family. Selena is now on that very short list too. For however long I have left in this world.

I keep my eyes locked with hers. Each tiny step she takes is another blow. It's all worth it if she walks out of here.

When she is finally—finally—near the door, I shift my gaze to Emmanuelle. I don't have to say the words. He's already moving to get to her.

He steps up behind her, his guards backing out the open door, already preparing to run. She tears her eyes from mine, her mouth drops open to say something, but Emmanuelle already has a hold of her.

She fights. Of course, she fights. There's no other way she'll leave me. I give him a nod in acknowledgment. Now it's not only Kai who owes him; it's me too.

He gives me one in turn, his arms clamped tight around Selena as he backs her out of the room. His guards surround them both. Once she's out of my sight, it's like something comes loose in my chest. A vital bolt holding everything together. I won't survive whatever Margery has in mind for me, so I won't let her get the chance.

I turn and face the first woman who ever paid for my flesh.

Now she'll pay with her life.

30

SELENA

I take back everything nice I've said or thought about Emmanuelle. Right now, I want to murder him. I thought he was on my side here, but now...he let me walk out of there without Michail and fucking fuck him.

I fight him. Scratch, kick, claw, anything to get free, but his arms are like iron bars around my midsection, and this frivolous dress is nothing but layers that impede my blows from being effective.

I croak out a curse, my throat raw. I've been screaming at him this entire time and not even realizing it. "Let me go. Let me go back to him."

Emmanuelle throws me into the back of an SUV and pushes in immediately after so I can't scramble around him. The opposite door is locked and won't open. I jab the button several more times and smack it. Nothing happens.

I have to get back to him. He shouldn't have to face this alone. Not when I'm the one who brought him here. He followed me, and now he's living out his worst nightmares. I swipe at the tears on my cheeks. My face is soaked, no doubt my makeup smeared, but none of it matters.

"Take me back," I whisper, still swiping my hands over the door to find a way out.

Emmanuelle sighs heavily and settles in the seat. "You know he wouldn't want you there. Taking you back is tantamount to killing you, and if that happened, I'd be next on the list of several people."

I leave the door and face him. "I can take care of myself. Take me back." I lace my tone with all the years I've been practicing at playing bitch queen.

He tilts his head, the look in his eyes asking, *Really?* "We are going back to your house so we can regroup and figure out a plan. An effective and safe plan to free Michail. I'm sure he'll be much better off if his friends and allies don't get murdered in his rescue attempt."

I throw myself back into the leather, crossing my arms. He rubs at the scratch marks on his hands and wrists, and I don't feel a single wisp of guilt. He deserved it. Just another man thinking he knows what's best for me.

We make it to my house in record time. The second the door opens, I'm ready to pop out, find a cab, and go back. But there's a guard twice Emmanuelle's size waiting to scoop me up and carry me in the townhouse.

He sets me on the hardwood floor of the foyer, and I shove him back when he releases his hands. "Don't you dare touch me again."

Emmanuelle enters behind him and sends his guards outside with a nod. "Stop acting like a child and think for a moment, and no one will have to put their hands on you."

It's on the tip of my tongue to tell him off again, but he's right. I'm being too emotional about this. Too attached. It's an easy way to get killed, or worse, Michail killed.

I head up the stairs, already stripping the stupid dress off my body. Emmanuelle follows but keeps his eyes averted as I enter my room in nothing but my underwear. He waits in the hall while I grab black leather pants, a t-shirt, and a jacket. Not my typical attire, but better than that damn cupcake dress I'd been wearing.

In the bathroom, I mop up my face with a makeup wipe and gather my hair into a messy bun. Again, not typical of my look, but all I need is the mess out of my face for now.

I find Emmanuelle standing in the hallway with his tuxedo jacket over his arm. "We should sit down and think about this."

No. He can sit and think about this. I'm arming myself, finding back up, and saving my man. And there is not a single person in the world brave enough to challenge me on that title right now. I nudge by him, shoulder checking on the way to the hallway closet, which doubles as my mini arsenal. My sister Julia set it up for when she's in town on a hunt. She won't mind one bit if I borrow some of her firepower to take out the usurper to our family seat.

But it's not about the council anymore. She made it personal when she took Michail. This is about how much of her brains I can blast all over the wall when I get to her.

My phone rings from somewhere, but I ignore it as I strap a knife to my boot and slip my arms into a holster.

Emmanuelle taps on my shoulder with the device and lets it slide over into my palm. It's an unknown number, so it might be anyone.

I hit the button. "Hello?"

"What the fuck do you think you're doing?" Kai's voice is harsh and muffled. A wrathful whisper.

I grit my teeth and dig through a bin of switchblades for my other boot. "Right now, I'm getting ready to storm our event space to get Michail back. Why, what are you doing?"

"Trying to make sure he gets out of there alive. No thanks to you."

I freeze, my hand on the stock of a sawed-off shotgun. "What do you know? How do you know? It just happened, and you weren't even there."

Again, he whispers into the phone, shooting static into my eardrums. "You don't need to concern yourself with it. I've been tracking all of your old council's movements, and tonight one popped on my radar."

"Margery?"

"Margery," he agrees. "But you need to stand down and let me deal with this."

I don't bother trying to keep my tone neutral. Not now, it's too late to go back. "We can't leave him there. She's twisted, insane, and I have no idea what she'll do to him the longer she has him." I swallow back a wave of nausea. "If she does what I assume she wants, then he won't make it back to me. He'll be broken in a way he doesn't even know yet."

There's a long pause, and I remember what others had said about Kai's own time in captivity. "I know firsthand what she could do to him. Trust me. I won't let my brother face something like that."

I don't want to wrap my brain around the possibilities. They are too disgusting to consider, and I wouldn't wish what Kai and Michail and probably so many other men have endured. Rape was never just a woman's issue.

My hands tremble as I close the closet door. Emmanuelle is standing against the wall a few feet away, no doubt filling in the blanks from Kai's side of the conversation. "Help me get him back, Kai. I know I don't deserve your help." I kept the details of my arrangement with that damn bitch councilwoman, Henrietta, to myself. She was supposed to free him, let him get on with his life. I took her word as the head of her council, and I learned my lesson the hard way.

Tears are falling again, and I tilt my head back and look up, trying to stifle them. "I don't deserve your help, but I need it. I need my family. I can't lose him, Kai."

There's no doubt in my mind I've confirmed how close Michail and I have really gotten over our forced time together. But it's a reckoning I can deal with after we save him.

More static cuts through the line, and then Kai rushes to speak in another whisper. "Head to the secondary council meeting space in one hour. Bring your fucking fiancé and his friends. They can help."

I click off, relief a flash of ice in my blood. It cools me down, calms me, lets the parts of my brain running on pure adrenaline gain control again.

Emmanuelle pushes off the wall. "What do you need?"

It's on the tip of my tongue to tell him to fuck off. That I can do this alone. Kai will help, and he's the only one I trust. Except, it's a lie. I might hate him for dragging me out of there, but now, on the other side of things, I see he did me a favor. I'd have likely died in that room if he hadn't hauled me away.

"Kai says to meet him at the secondary council location in one hour."

He tilts his head, studying my face. "And you know where that is, I assume?"

I nod and tuck the phone into my knife-filled pocket. "Gather your guys. They can come too."

For a heartbeat, he stays and stares at me. I worry he's going to refuse, extricate himself to go back to his own council and his own people. He doesn't need to be involved in this, not when we both know our relationship is a sham.

Then he turns and heads down the stairs two at a time with his long legs, and I'm left alone with way more feelings than I'm comfortable with. The urge to get a drink and relax beats at me, but I can't risk it. Not with Michail needing me. Not with Kai counting on me. Not with Emmanuelle waiting for me.

My clothes are bulky as I descend to the first floor. When I get to the foyer, I remove a few of the knives and keep the ones at my ankles and one on my forearm. Seeing as I've been trained for politics, I've never really had to defend myself. There were always guards, or others, who would intervene if something happened. But growing up with Julia and Kai means I know how to use the weapons I've loaded myself with. I've kept my skills sharp, as Julia likes to randomly attack me to keep me on my toes when she's in town. I call it lurid. She calls it sisterly bonding.

I grab some water, watching the clock. Not long now before we can leave. I hate every second which passes with him in her clutches.

One of Emmanuelle's guards enters the kitchen. He's changed from his suit to a black-on-black outfit similar to my own, except cargos instead of leather. I study all his pockets. "Smart, you can carry more weapons in those."

He gives me a toothy grin. "True, but my ass doesn't look nearly as good in these as yours does in those."

I roll my eyes and follow him back out to the foyer. He has no interest in me, any more than I have in him, but soldiers walking into battle need something to connect over. Emmanuelle waits by the door in his own black-on-black ensemble. I guess we have a color scheme tonight. Julia, with her all-black wardrobe, would be so proud.

If Emmanuelle hadn't mentioned he was into Andrea, I might have tried to hook him up with my sister. Once we end our fake engagement, of course.

I clench my fists, stretching my fingers and wrists, while Emmanuelle keeps an eye on his watch.

The second we can leave he turns and walks out, expecting all of us to follow. He can think he's in charge all he wants as long as I can bring Michail home in one piece.

We climb into the vehicle, and one of Emmanuelle's oversized goons drives. I note the four others that climb into the other vehicle.

"Did you feed them some kind of human growth serum to get them that big?"

He rolls his face toward me, devoid of humor. "Funny. Very funny. Who knew you get funny when you're about to walk into a fight?"

I shrug. "I get horny, too, but that's not something I'm going to let you handle."

Now he chuckles, facing out the window again. "No, you're right. Michail would cut off my cock, and I'm rather attached to it."

On that upbeat note, we lapse into silence, each of us preparing mentally for the battle to come.

31

MICHAIL

Margery runs her hand around from the back of my neck over my shoulder. I've had enough of people touching me without my permission. Enough of women thinking they own me because I happen to be good looking and it's their right.

I give the empty doorway one more longing glance and face Margery.

She's smiling now, completely focused on me. In her mind, she's already won, and Selena isn't a threat.

In her hubris, she's forgotten who I am...even though she knew all along that I'm a member of the Five. She assumed because I have a pretty face and gave her a well-choreographed act I'm not just as dangerous as my counterparts. That I'm not more dangerous.

Some of the men in the room shift in their seats. They haven't forgotten who I am.

I'm the shadows which reach out and take a bite when you least expect it. I'm the one Adrian sends when subtlety and finesse have gone out the window.

Margery reaches up to wind her arms around my neck, and I'm already moving, angling my hands to either side of her head like I might kiss her. She's been waiting, hinting about kissing me all evening. It never occurs to her I have other plans.

She closes her eyes, and I'm almost at the right angle to snap her little twig neck when hands land on my shoulders, pulling me off.

The fucking guards haven't forgotten who I am either, it would seem. I fight as they wrestle me off my feet. I glimpse a man's stubble, and the glint of a pin on his turtleneck, as I land on my knees hard. Pain shoots up into my thighs, cascading through my body. It seems to last forever thanks to whatever drugs Margery gave me.

I move to drop the tie on my wrists, the one I loosened, but one of the guards on me is there first. He jerks the rope tight, so it cuts into my wrists. "What the hell, asshole? Is it necessary to tie it that tight?"

He doesn't respond, and I imagine crushing his jugular with my favorite pair of boots. "Love the outfits, boys. Really sets the Dungeons-R-Us vibe. You even have the little club pin and everything."

One of the guards knees me in the kidney, and I fold over, struggling against the pain.

Margery speaks up from where she's resumed her place on her throne. "Oh, don't hurt him too badly. I want him to be functional when we get to the old council seat."

At least if they are moving me, she can't come back here and be dragged into this mess. It's a relief, even if I have no idea where their council hosts their regular meetings. I assumed this was it since it's the only place I've seen images of.

When I can sit up again, Margery slinks off her throne toward me. I have to actually try to keep the bile down.

She cups my cheeks in her cold brittle fingers, leaning in. "You were so sweet earlier. Can't we go back to that?"

I consider. Since my brain is moving way too slowly, I'm not sure any acting on my part will go over well. So I shrug. "I'm not against being nice to you as long as you are nice to me."

She soothes her thumb over my bottom lip, and I jerk forward, snapping my teeth. I barely miss her, sending her backward so quickly she lands on her ass.

Good, now she knows how my knees feel right now.

She waves at the guards who haul me to my feet, the others closing ranks around us as we exit. The event hall is deserted. Broken glass shimmers on the floor where party goers left in a rush. I can't blame them. Or maybe I can when it's them who've accepted this woman as their leader. As if she's even in the same league as Selena. If the rest of the council thinks that, then they are even more delusional than I thought.

I'm roughly tossed into the back of her town car. Two guards sit in the front seat and one in the back. With my hands still tied, I don't have much of a chance to escape, even if this would have been the best place to attempt it.

I settle into the seat, shifting uncomfortably around my bound hands. "Hey, one of you guys want to untie me? What if I pinky swear I won't try to run away?"

One of the front seat guards chuckles softly. The other two remain silent and completely ignore me.

We leave, and I keep careful tabs out the window on where we are headed. If Margery were smart, she would have blindfolded me, put headphones over my ears, done everything in her power to ensure I couldn't lead someone to wherever she intends to take me. Well, it will only matter if I can get out of here alive. Right now, my odds aren't looking so hot.

I pick at the knots around my wrist, but they are tight as hell and not budging. So instead, I focus on the guards. They are all still wearing their ski masks, as if they aren't people so much as goons for hire. I try goading them. "Hey, is that face thing hot? It looks hot? I won't tell if you take it off, roll down the window, cool off. You've been working hard today; you deserve a break."

I didn't keep the sarcasm out of my tone. They all sit silently in response. Interesting. Who knew Selena's council had such interesting guards? Or maybe they are Margery's personal guard. There's no way to tell.

It only takes about ten minutes to get to our destination. "Where are we?" I try. Of course, not a peep from the goon squad as they jerk me from the car and lead me into a warehouse type of building.

Inside looks very similar to the event space with the marble columns, but the outside of the place is built like a ring, not unlike the chairs in the other place. Except this one has a door at each point a chair would sit.

It looks like the set of a mythological game show. What's behind door number two?

They lead me to the one dead center of the curve, no doubt the room meant for the lead councilmember. When we get to the door, one guard shoves it open while the others toss me inside.

My hip hits the edge of some kind of furniture. The room is pitch black, so I stumble around until I find a clear spot to sit on the floor and consider my options.

It smells clean in here. Freshly clean, not like the councilwoman's perfume or anything. So maybe she didn't use this room much and intends to keep me as a prisoner. Ransom could be considered if she weren't so hell bent on sleeping with me.

It's dark, and I can't hear anything outside the room. Nothing within either. No beep or lights from electronics, or even a fan.

I don't know how long has passed when the door opens to reveal my captor in a beam of light. I duck my chin to protect my eyes as she flips the light switch. "Why are you sitting here in the dark?"

Really? That's her question? It's dumb as fuck, so I don't give her an answer.

She crosses the room, which is longer than my original estimation, and sits on the bed with a little bounce. She'd changed since we arrived, now wearing a dress even worse than her previous one. Even though she is getting older, she's trying to pretend she's not. There's nothing less attractive on a woman than this level of insecurity. It's not even normal does-this-dress-make-me-look-fat insecurity. Which explains why I'm here, tied up, about to be used for whatever perverted fantasy she has playing in her mind.

She pats the bed beside her. "You can come sit with me. You might be more comfortable."

I shake my head and tent my knees to rest my elbows on top. "I'm good right here."

When she pouts and bats her lashes, I almost wish I joined her so I could slap that fucking look off her face. "What is wrong with you? Why did you kidnap me?"

She straightens, all pretense at allure wiped off her now shrewd features. Ah, so she's at least somewhat of a good actress then. Interesting. "That's an easy one...because you belong to me, and Selena took you."

"You took over her council seat way before I came into her life. Hell, you're the one who drove us together since I had to keep her safe."

She scowls, slumping like a petulant teenager. "Don't remind me. A miscalculation on my part. She's always refused help in the past. I thought she'd rush off to her home, and I could send my men to take her out easily. Selena is not known for playing well with others."

I study this woman, trying to pinpoint where she's going with this. "Why though? Why now? Why not make a bid for the chair when her parent's abdicated?"

Margery stands and sidles closer, swinging her hips as if she can entice me. The guards step up and lift me to stand, then drag me to the bed. I roll and try to get up, but a sharp bite in my neck stops me cold. Another dose of drugs. Fucking great. What is she going to do to me while I'm out? No. I can't let this happen. I swing my tied wrists around and roll, attempting to rise, stand. Hopefully upright, maybe I can do something. But all I manage is to rock back and forth, the room spinning around me.

I feel a weight on my lap and open my eyes, which I didn't even remember closing, to see her straddle me. Thankfully, she's still clothed, but I hate her contact with me all the same.

"No," I say, trying to lift my hips to dislodge her.

Margery tuts, pressing down harder on my hips. Digging her weight in. "Calm down, Beautiful. We have a long night ahead of us, and I don't want you worn out too soon."

Bile rises in my throat again, and I roll my face to the side, so I don't puke all over myself. I hack and spit, but nothing else. When I lie back again, panting, she's frozen, standing over me, a look of disgust on her face.

I glare. "What? You don't want me now that you've seen your presence makes me sick? Ask me why. Come on, Margery. Ask me why all I can think about right now is carving out your miserable, dead heart."

Her voice trembles, shooting satisfaction through me. "Wh-why?"

The drugs are already settling in, and my mind feels so hazy at the edges. Once upon a time, I would have lived every day in this dreamy state. Not now, not with the memories of what she did to me, what she carved into me, so fresh. "Once upon a time, about eight years or so ago, you went for a little shopping trip. Do you remember what you bought?"

She stares in confusion and slides off my lap to sit on the bed.

With her weight gone, some of my sanity leeches back in. But it's too late. One of us is going to die here tonight.

She doesn't answer, so I continue as if she had. "You bought a scared, scrawny, starved sixteen-year-old boy in a cage. Do you remember that?"

Her eyes fly wide. "But...you're dead. They told me you died."

I meet her eyes and spit in her shocked face. "I did die that day. Trust me. Everything in that boy is gone now, thanks to you and your friends."

32

SELENA

My hands shake as we get closer and closer to the meeting point. I shove them under my thighs to keep them still. If she's touched him...If she's hurt him...

"Is it up ahead?" Emmanuelle asks.

I glance over at him, trying to focus on what he said. "Oh, yes, it's around the warehouse ahead. The farthest in the lot."

We drive farther, only to stop short as three of the council guards step into the middle of the road.

I crane my neck to get a look between the front seats. "Shit. How did they know we were coming? Do you think she bugged my phone?" Her only chance would have been at lunch that day we caught up. But I didn't notice anything. Not that I had been looking for something suspicious.

We slow to a stop. The other vehicle too. Then it's all-out chaos between the guards' guns and Emmanuelle's goons.

I step out of the car, keeping to the side of it in case anyone wants to earn a pay bump by taking me out. As I get closer, I notice these three guards are wearing pins on their turtlenecks, and one is a woman. So far, there hasn't been a single woman hired for the guard, and I know because I do the hiring.

"Excuse me," I call from behind the safety of the vehicle. "Who are you?"

I hear a deep masculine laugh and know it immediately.

Kai.

He strips the ski mask over his head and rubs at the top, where it's sticking up at odd angles. "I was hoping you'd figure it out. We've been here the whole time."

I step around the car, march straight up to him, and slap him so hard my hands hurts,

The person next to him, still wearing a mask, grabs my arms to pull me away from him. I jerk from his grasp, giving him a glare all of his own. "You let her just take him? You could have killed them all. Anyone who wasn't with you. And she wouldn't be doing God knows what to him right now..." I trail off as a hot tear slides down my cheek.

The man releases me, another set of arms goes around me, and I'm face-first in a solid chest. Kai holds me tight for a few seconds until I get my composure back and then releases me. "We had to let her take him. We needed to find her base of operations. Especially where she keeps her servers."

"What servers? What are you talking about?"

The third person, Andrea, I assume, strips her mask off, and somehow, she is just as perfect as usual. She steps up and answers my question. "We've been working to take out the Capri family for a while now. Ever since Adrian met Valentina. Sal, one of the heirs to the Capri family, was her fiancé. He's super dead now."

Kai snickers a bit, and we all swing our gazes back to him. "What? That piece of shit deserved it. So now, we are taking on this end of the Capri operations. They send out illegal porn and images to those who might now want to purchase an entire human being."

Nausea rises, and I grab his arm to steady myself. She's with him right now. "We have to get in there and get him out. I don't want him in there longer than necessary."

Kai nods and jerks his ski mask back on. The others as well. "We are going to lead you in like we caught you sneaking around. When we have an opening, we'll make a move to kill the other guards. You get to Michail while I destroy the servers."

Seems like a reasonable plan. There are so many ways this could go wrong. But we have backup. That's better than nothing. I nod once and put my hands behind my back for him to zip tie. He does it quickly but leaves enough room that I can slip my hands out easily.

"I'm going to be extra bitchy to you in particular," I say.

That makes him chuckle as everyone else goes over the plan and gets tied. They lead us in a line, at gunpoint, into the warehouse. This used to be the old council meeting place. Now, most of the time, we meet at the event center since it was easier, as most of our meetings occurred during events.

Kai leads us around the center of the room toward a bedroom in the far back, the one corresponding to my chair. This fucking bitch.

When we stop, Kai speaks to a guard outside the door quickly. The guard disappears into the room, and in a second Margery exits, a wicked wide grin on her face. "You came to join us, after all."

I want to wrap my hands around her throat right here, but I can't risk it, not with Michail still in there in Lord knows what shape. "Where is he?"

"Resting after our time together."

She's changed, but she doesn't look like she's been at Michail's mercy. Trust me. It leaves a mark. "You're lying. He doesn't want you while drugged any more than he does sober."

Kai steps around us, and I glance out of the corner of my eye. He gives a subtle nod that even I understand. *Keep her distracted while he slips into the room to check on him.*

"So, is this about him, or me, or did you just want my job from the very beginning? Why didn't you run like every other candidate?"

Her smile is gone, and her eyes flash fire. "Everyone knew you didn't actually run. You were Mommy and Daddy's perfect child. Destined to take the throne when they abdicated. No one could have run against you."

A gun shot makes me jump. Her eyes fly toward the door behind me, and then everything jumbles together really quickly, like a movie on fast forward.

Kai exits the room with his arm propped around Michail. Andrea and the other man from outside swing around to take out the guards. A couple of other guards close in on their friends from behind until the only ones left standing are the ones with the pins on their shirts. Absurdly, I feel the need to count them all. Five in total, which means wearing one of these masks is the infamous Adrian Doubeck, in the flesh. Someone like him came for Michail too?

The guards with pins on our side of the room split off and join us. The others stare around, confused, until Kai raises his voice. "If you don't want to be lined up against that wall and shot, you better walk out of here right now."

The extra guards flee, except the ones nearest us.

He doesn't answer, and I spin to look at the rest of the guards who crowd in close. They've stripped their masks to reveal every member of Michail's team. Even Adrian has folded himself into an empty council chair, looking every inch a king on his throne.

I stare down at the woman. Someone I thought was my friend. She's never been a particularly nice person, but I didn't think she could be capable of what is racing through my head. Of what Kai told me.

No. How could I have missed it?

One of the guards who had been waiting for us to return walks calmly through the group, a gun held barrel first in his hand. When he reaches Michail, he strips off his mask one-handed and wraps Michail's fingers around the stock of the gun. They share something for a moment, and I step back to line up with the other guards. This is something he needs to do for himself.

"You won't just shoot me like—"

Her words are cut off as Michail fires the gun. She crumples, her thin frame folding in on itself until she hits the floor. I guess he had nothing else to say to her.

I don't give a shit about her. All I care about is him. But he looks calm, collected, his usual mask.

Adrian rounds on all of us. "Anyone have a problem with this?"

Of course, no one utters a word. I rush to Michail's side and wrap myself around his middle. "Are you okay? Are you hurt? Did she do anything to you?"

His arms close around me just as hard, and I squeeze him back.

Kai shouts from across the room where there is a line of computers. "I've got this. You guys get out of here. It won't take me very long."

I stare around at these people. Michail's family. They saved him; they saved us. Emmanuelle and his guys have already disappeared, and I didn't even get to thank him.

I shift my focus to Adrian. "Thank you."

He tilts his head, regarding me, and under the heavy weight of his gaze, I get the feeling he finds me lacking. "We saved you because you're Kai's sister and he asked me to. End of story. Also, Andrea will join your council."

It's not a question, but a command. Since I owe him my life, and Michail's, I don't argue...this time. "How did you guys get in here?"

A man I assume is Andrea's brother, Alexei, sits in one of the council seats in the center of the floor, wiggling to test it out. "This is really uncomfortable. To answer your question, Emmanuelle set it up easily enough. He has connections everywhere, apparently."

I guess I owe him more than I thought I did. But why the ruse of the engagement? My mind circles back to Andrea. Maybe he wanted to make her jealous and do whatever he had planned at the same time. Not that he and I ever did anything that would make someone jealous.

Adrian heads toward the door. "Let's go." He takes a step, stops, and turns back. "Grab that bitch on the floor. I want to send her back to her fucking friends."

We follow Adrian out. The entire place is deserted and some part of me wants to burn the building to the ground to scrub out the taint Margery brought to it.

Adrian and his team climb into a black SUV, leaving Kai, me, and Michail with the other.

We sit in the car, all silently taking things in.

Michail breaks it, his voice pitched low. "I guess you got your council back."

I stare at him, trying to figure out what he's not saying. It hits me. No. Fucking no. I refuse to let him do this. I close the distance between us, grab his face, and tug him down to meet me. "Don't you fucking dare pull that you're better off without me crap right now, because I will knee you in the balls."

Kai shifts nearby, and I throw him a look, still holding onto Michail's face. "Can I help you?"

He narrows his eyes right back. "Oh, we are fucking talking about this at a later date. For now, I'll give you two some privacy, so I don't have to witness something that might scar me for life."

I keep Michail's face in my hands and press my forehead to his the entire drive to my house. Kai leaves immediately with a warning he'll be back, and I heft Michail up to help him inside. He seems fine physically, but the drugs she gave him makes him unsteady on his feet.

When the front door closes, I focus on Michail again. "I'm not joking right now."

"They came for me," he whispers. When his knees give out and he hits the hardwood, I go down with him.

I hug him closer and shake my head. "It doesn't matter now. I just wish I'd known. Why didn't you tell me?"

He meets my eyes head on, nothing but him in there. No masks. No acts. A pure and shining connection I can feel through every inch of my body. "My trauma isn't something I talk about. And it's not your job to heal me. I've done all the healing I can do up to this point. The rest takes time. And a lot of bullets in pedophiles' brains."

While I want to know all of him, the darkness, and the light, he's absolutely right. His trauma isn't something he has to share with anyone, and I can respect that. "I would have shot her in the head at lunch that day if I'd known. How could you just sit there and pretend it didn't affect you? Today even, too?"

A corner of his lips tilts up. "I'm very good at what I do."

It's my turn to smile, and I climb over the dress to straddle him in nothing but my underwear and heels. "And what do you do?"

He runs his lips down the column of neck and bites gently on my shoulder. "Babysit, apparently."

I chuckle, wrap my arms around his head, and hold him against me. He moves to the other side of my neck, trailing kisses and leaving bites.

"I hate you," he whispers into my skin. "So much."

There's a rawness to his tone which hollows me out. As if even saying those words are too much when we both know exactly what they mean. Of course, he'd feel vulnerable, exposed. Margery stripped away everything he uses to hide himself, protect himself, even from me.

But I can give it back if he wants it. If he needs it. I can deal with the masks if it means I have him healthy and whole.

I drop my head back, trying to give him all the access I possibly can. His teeth graze my skin, shooting sensation everywhere in a white-hot flash. "I hate you too." It's more of a pant as I succumb to the feeling of his lips on my skin.

He eases me off his lap and strips off the pieces of his tuxedo one by one. It's not sexy but methodical.

I remember she put him in that suit. She dressed him up for her own pleasure.

I attack his shoes, his socks, helping him kick away the pants until he's gloriously naked on my hardwood floor. His curls fall unruly around his face, and I shove them back over the crown of his head gently.

"You're mine."

He nods. "And you're mine."

I shimmy enough to get out of my underwear and bra, then climb back onto his lap again. When his warm skin meets mine, I sigh against his mouth. "My brother is going to make you pay for this."

"Let's skip talking about your brother for now. I need to be inside you." He lifts my hips to rearrange me so he's nudging at my entrance. I'm not very wet yet, and for a second, the stretch is almost painful as he slowly lowers me onto him. But I don't have to worry. He thumbs my clit and holds me around the waist until I'm panting and sliding along his length easier.

"You're mine," he repeats. This time it sounds darker, deeper. As if it's more than words alone.

I'm too breathless to say anything, so I simply nod, grasping his shoulders for leverage. He's filling me so completely in this position, I can barely think straight. I tentatively rock forward, testing the sensation. When I shift my hips back some, the angle causes a delicious friction inside me, lighting me up, setting my nerves on fire.

"Yes," I whisper.

He continues to work my clit with one hand, keeping me steady while I move with the other. It only takes a few minutes for me to climb the peak and throw myself over the top. He comes with me, his mouth on my neck, his teeth in my skin prolonging my orgasm in a dichotomy of pleasure and pain so deep, it threatens to swallow me whole.

When we stop moving, our panting breaths mingling, I press my forehead to his. "You're mine," I whisper.

He nods, his lids heavy, no doubt still fighting some of whatever that bitch drugged him with.

I wobble to my feet and pull him up with me. We shower together quickly, climb into bed, and I fold myself against his side.

He wraps his arm around me, his hand on my ass in a claiming grip.

We stay that way in the dark quiet room, listening to each other breathe. "I know we have a lot to figure out," he whispers after so long that I thought he was asleep.

"Yes."

He smooths his hand over my bare waist as if testing I'm still there. "I love you, Selena. I have since the moment you didn't argue with me in the elevator the first time. You slipped into that mask so beautifully, and every time after. You're incredible."

I'm not sure what to say to that. "I love you, too. But I don't want masks, or acts, between us. I want just us, but if that's what you need, then I'm here for you. Any way. Every way you'll let me be."

He kisses the top of my head, and it's enough. There's not a doubt in my mind he knows how hard it is for me to admit how much I need him.

I close my eyes and snuggle into him, letting the soothing scent of lemongrass carry me off to sleep.

EPILOGUE

Selena
Two months later...
The Doubeck Penthouse

I stare down at a tiny piece of plastic that has just changed my entire life.

Gently, I place it beside the six other identical pieces of plastic on the countertop.

After the events in Chicago, I took my seat on the council again, but this time, determined to root out the rot which had somehow leached into my society.

We aren't good people. We aren't kind people. But we don't buy and sell humans. That I won't allow in my territory.

And while I know it's a worthy crusade, some small part of me knew I'd lose Michail if I didn't at least try. Now we split our time between my townhouse and the penthouse. It's a good thing someone's boss owns a helicopter.

Staring at the pregnancy tests only makes my decision easier. Children need to be protected. In our world, they so often aren't.

I run my hand over my still flat stomach and text Andrea, who's become a friend after everything. She doesn't answer, but a knock comes from my door a moment later.

But the knock is perfunctory. She walks right in before I call out.

When she finds me in the bathroom, she spots the tests, then looks at me, and then back at the tests. "You peed on those, and you're putting them there where you brush your teeth?"

I huff, rush over, and drag her closer.

She jerks her arm from my hold. "I hope you washed your hands."

"Would you shut up and look at these?"

"They all say: pregnant."

I stare, hoping she's right and she's wrong at the same time. "Are you sure?"

She points to one without touching it, her silky hair sliding over her shoulder. "Yeah. See...P-R-E-G-N-A-N-T. It's not like those red line ones. It clearly says it. Uh...six...no seven times. So I think that's pretty conclusive."

My stomach rolls, and I race to the toilet. This has been happening for a few weeks now, but I didn't think it was possible. I've been on birth control since I was sixteen. Even though I'd never had sex, Mom feared I'd get pregnant early and ruin my chances of taking over the council. Well...I've been on birth control since I was sixteen...minus several weeks I got locked into a hotel with a ridiculously gorgeous man for my protection.

Bet she never had that situation on her radar. I wonder how she'll feel about becoming a grandmother.

Andrea scoops my hair back, holding it while I finish in the bathroom. After I wash my hands, under her supervision, she hands me a glass of water.

"You okay?"

I swallow thickly, my throat dry. "Yes. I think so. Maybe. No."

She snorts. "Clears that right up then. Do you want me to go get Michail?"

Shit. I guess I should tell him. I'm not sure what he's going to say, or think, about this. We've never discussed it. Never even brought it up.

I nod once. Might as well get it over with. If I don't, then I'll regret it. Andrea goes to leave, and I spot something in my jewelry dish. Quickly, I swipe it up, chase after her into the main suite, and press it into her palm.

She stares down at the engagement ring Emmanuelle gave me. "Oh, well, I mean if Michail wouldn't murder me, sure, I'll marry you."

I meet her eyes, knowing the false humor she forces into her tone is just her way of keeping people from asking the hard questions she doesn't want to answer. "I think this belongs to you. It never belonged to me."

She stares down at it for several seconds, then slides it in the pocket of her black slacks. "You don't know everything about him. We could never be together anyway. Besides, I hate him."

It didn't look like that to me, but she doesn't give me the chance to comment, walking away to find Michail.

I head back into the bathroom, rubbing my hands down my green pencil skirt. He enters at almost a run, his face lined with his worry. "What is it? Are you okay? What's wrong?"

I clear my throat and glance pointedly at the countertop.

He settles his shoulders back, his face going carefully blank, as he looks the tests over. "How do you feel about this?"

I'm waiting for some kind of reaction from him, but he's giving me absolutely nothing. "Scared, maybe. I'm too young to be a mother."

"Valentina is younger than you, and you can already see her little bump."

It's on the tip of my tongue to point out that Valentina wasn't trained to run a criminal empire, but I don't. That's the old me. The one who made everything about herself. I take a deep breath and let it trickle out slowly. "I think I'm okay with this."

He captures my face between his palms, searching my eyes. "What does okay mean? You want to keep it?"

I jerk back, his words burning unexpectedly, but he doesn't release me. "What do you mean? You thought I'd want to…"

Something bright enters his eyes. "I didn't know, and it's your decision. It's always your choice, but I can't lie and say it wouldn't have broken my heart."

Tears well up in my eyes, slipping over. He swipes them away with his thumbs. "So you are excited?" I whisper.

He nods and then presses his head to mine. "Of course I am. Babies are great, and they smell so good."

I laugh at the absurdity of his statement, but can't refute it. "Then I guess we are having a baby."

He laughs, picking me up in his arms. I hold on to his neck, my skirt keeping me from gripping him with my legs.

I kiss him, demanding and rough. His groan is interrupted by a knock.

We pull apart to find Kai standing in the doorway, glaring at us. His eyes stray to the tests on the counter, but he only says, "Command center, now, both of you. We have a situation."

We follow him to the command center. The table is full, so we stand at the side, holding hands, to watch the TV blaring loudly through the room.

"FBI Agent Manny Molina was arrested today under suspicion of multiple charges… They aren't releasing the…"

Adrian flicks off the TV and stares at the table in front of him. His tone is carefully neutral. Too calm. "Who knew Emmanuelle was FBI?"

Kai, Andrea, and Alexei all step forward. He waves at them, his jaw tense. "Explain before I lose my shit."

As usual, Kai takes the lead. "He might be FBI, but I believe he's come to our side. They've been hunting Sal's family, the Capri's, as well. That's why he was installed as an undercover agent. He got mixed up in an incident..." He glances pointedly at Andrea, then back to Adrian. "...which he disagreed with. He's on our side now."

Valentina reaches over and rubs the top of Adrian's shoulders, saying nothing, but visibly bringing him down from whatever edge he's dancing on. "How do you know he wasn't playing us?"

I clamp my mouth shut. Everything I saw in the man told me he'd been sincere.

Adrian presses his fist to the table and then stands abruptly, sending us all backward out of the way. "I want a report on all of this. Immediately. It's time for the next step."

He sweeps Valentina in his arms, bridal style, and walks out of the room, leaving the rest of us in stunned silence.

Kai drops into the empty chair and tugs his laptop in front of him.

I can't take the questions anymore. "What's the next step?"

"Now, we play the FBI like a fucking fiddle to destroy the Capri family for good."

Check out more of our books here.

ABOUT THE AUTHORS

J.L. Beck is a *USA Today* and international bestselling author who writes contemporary and dark romance. She is also one half of the author duo Beck & Hallman. Check out her Website to order Signed Paperbacks and special swag.

www.bleedingheartromance.com

Monica Corwin is a New York Times and USA Today Bestselling author. She is an outspoken writer attempting to make romance accessible to everyone, no matter their preferences. As a Northern Ohioian, Monica enjoys snow drifts, three seasons of weather, and a dislike of Michigan football. Monica owns more books about King Arthur than should be strictly necessary. Also typewriters...lots and lots of typewriters.

You can find her on Facebook, Instagram and Twitter or check out her website.

www.monicacorwin.com

Printed in Great Britain
by Amazon